SOUND

MAYA DANIELS

Vinci Books

vinci-books.com

Published by Vinci Books Ltd in 2026

Copyright © Maya Daniels 2020

The author has asserted their moral right to be identified as the author of this work in accordance with the Copyright, Designs and Patents Act 1988. This work is a work of fiction. Names, characters, places and incidents are the product of the author's imagination or are used fictitiously. Any resemblance to actual persons, living or dead, places and incidents is entirely coincidental.

All rights reserved. No part of this publication may be copied, reproduced, distributed, stored in any retrieval system, or transmitted in any form or by any means, including photocopying, recording, or other electronic or mechanical methods, nor used as a source for any form of machine learning including AI datasets, without the prior written permission of the publisher.

The publisher and the author have made every effort to obtain permissions for any third party material used in this book and to comply with copyright law. Any queries in this respect should be brought to the attention of the publisher and any omissions will be corrected in future editions.

A CIP catalogue record for this book is available from the British Library.

Paperback ISBN: 9781036705916

The EU GPSR authorised representative is Logos Europe, 9 rue Nicolas Poussion, 17000 La Rochelle, France contact@logoseurope.eu

By Maya Daniels

The Last Note Series
Sound
Sonata

The Necronomicon Guardian
The Magician
The High Priestess

Chronicles of Forbidden Witchery Series
Resting Witch Face
Pitch a Witch
Witch Please
Payback is a Witch

The Broken Halos Series
The Devil is in the Details
Speak of the Devil
Encounter with the Devil
The Devil in Disguise
To Look the Devil in the Eye
Better The Devil You Know
Give a Devil His Due

Hidden Portals Trilogy

Venus Trap

The First Secret

Daywalker Series

Investigated

Infiltrated

Instigated

Initiated

Infuriated

Ignited

Infernal Regions for the Unprepared

Black Hand

Lower World

Everlasting Fire

Place of Torment

Hellfire To Come

The Courtless Fae Series

Secret Origins

New Blood Rising

Rebirth - Risorgimento

Overthrown - Rovesciamento

Recognition - Riconoscimento

The Gatekeepers Legacy

Legacy of Water

Legacy of Fire

Legacy of Spirit

Honor Among Thieves

Stolen Magic

Stolen Oath

By Maya Daniels

The Cursed Kingdom

Prologue

"Where are you going Melody?" Leaning against the doorframe, my mother watches me move around the room, no inflection in her tone when she speaks. Her hair is dull, hanging limply over her bony shoulders, adding to the washed away look of her wrinkled, faded clothing. That dress has seen much better days, but she won't take it off for anything. "I told you its better if you don't play that cursed instrument, didn't I? Isn't that why you stopped?"

"It's just one audition, Mom. I told you Vi and Harmony want to try, so I'll just keep them company this one time." Gently pulling out my violin from the case, I check it over. The moment I realize it isn't broken, my knees buckle. I didn't know how worried I was until just now that I broke it.

Last night, two jerks had grabbed my arm and tried forcing me to dance with them. Waiting patiently for Vi to talk to her sister—the bartender in the club—I breathed through my mouth so I didn't puke from all the harsh perfumes and sweat. I knew the guys were drunk and I had no idea what possessed me, but when I told one of them I didn't dance, he called me a bitch. It set me off and before I knew what is happening, he was on the ground unconscious while the bones in my arms vibrated from the strength used to whack him with my violin case. His buddy suffered the same fate, too.

And then he came.

The blue-eyed guy that made me toss and turn all night, stealing my sleep.

I can still hear his deep voice like he is talking inside my head. Like every hot-blooded woman, I've seen my fair share of good-looking guys. The ones that you need to do a double take on to make sure what you see is right, and not a trick your mind is playing on you. This one is in a league all on his own, though. There is something about him apart from being so pretty, but I'm not sure I can put my finger on it.

Last night, I stared at him, blinking stupidly for a few moments before I could find my voice to speak. It wasn't that, however, that made him different. It was a feeling that ran deep inside like I knew him, or at least should know him.

Thinking about it today, it's stupid and wrong on so many levels.

"Are you listening?" my mother drones on, clearing the image of the hot guy from my head.

"Yes, and I'm going to play today regardless of what I think or what you say. It'll be just one song anyway." Placing the violin back in the case, I close it by snapping the locks shut. Glancing out the window I see a car pulling up in front of the house. "Ah, there is Vi."

The blaring coming out from the car sounds like a football horn while Viola keeps hitting the heels of her palm on it, just like she always does. Seeing her lowering the passenger window lights a fire under my ass to get out of here. Grabbing my instrument, I whirl out of the room, kissing my mom on the cheek on my way out. Her deep sigh, very telling that the level of her depression has hit rock bottom, is like a knife in my chest. I want to do something, say something that will make her feel better, but since the day my father left, nothing ever seems to cheer her up.

She blames me for it.

I was young but I remember the nights hearing him yell at her or call her names. He wasn't physically abusive, but words sometimes hurt more than a slap on the face. When he packed up and left that day, I blamed myself because every time I heard him do that I covered my head with a blanket whispering, "Go away and leave us alone." My voice sounding strange to my ears. Guilt ate me alive while growing up but eventually I got over it.

Until one day while upset my mother threw it in my face. She screamed at me, blaming my cursed tongue for sending him away and forcing her to take care of me by herself. She still blames me now, even when she doesn't say the words. I stopped talking much to her in general.

Maybe she is right and I did send him packing. If my music can kill people, why can't my voice chase them away from me?

Backtracking, I shake off the gloomy thoughts and give my mother a one-arm hug, kissing her sunken cheek firmly with a smack. I giggle when she tries to get away. "Love you mom. I'll be back before you know it."

Releasing her, a shiver like I just walked over a fresh grave slithers up my spine when I hear my mom say, 'No you won't." But that's insane. Why on earth would she say something morbid like that? I blame my lack of sleep and my raging hormones—which are still going nuts from the blue-eyed guy—for making me little nuts.

"About time," Vi yells through her open window when I jump over the few steps at the front door. "You are like a geriatric patient, shuffling instead of walking. Chop chop, sweet ass, we don't want to be late."

"Stop yelling like a crazy person; the entire neighborhood can hear you."

Climbing in the back seat, I hug my violin case while leaning over to see my mom standing at the threshold staring at us will those dull eyes. The woman must have a couple of wires crossed talking about random powers, magic, and other stuff I can only shake my head at. Forcing a bright smile, I wave enthusiastically at her, but she doesn't move.

"Your mom okay?" Murmuring, Vi locks gazes with me through the rearview mirror.

"Unless I'm going nuts, I think I heard her tell me *'no you won't'* when I said I'll be back before you know it."

"It's the depression talking." With a sad smile, Vi peels off the sidewalk heading for Harmony's house. "That's why I can't wait for the three of us to get a house together. It'll remove all the crazy from our lives."

"Yeah." Sighing, I melt into the back seat and lean my head against it, closing my eyes.

"You dreamed about the hottie from the club didn't you." She kept calling him hottie on our way home from the club, too.

"I was sleeping like the dead. No hotties in my dreams." Lying to your friends is not the best course of action, but I'll never hear the end of it otherwise. Not that omitting the truth will work on Viola. The woman is like a bloodhound.

"Liar, liar, pants on fire," Vi sing songs, confirming my

Sound

thoughts "Your face is bright red. You did dream of him you hoe!"

"Hey! No name calling." I stick my tongue out at her. "And no slut shaming, either." we both burst into laughter.

"I have a feeling you'll see him again." Another of those shivers rattles my bones. What is it with people and saying sentences like they're premonitions or something? Geez, I can't catch a break.

"Yes, I'm sure I will. In some movie or something." I see Vi shrug a shoulder before I turn to watch the houses and trees pass by the window. "What would someone like him do with a girl as plain and unassuming as me?" The words are just a breath under my nose.

I hope the day will get better than it is right now.

Chapter One

Melody

My hand trembles when I lift the glass to my lips, the water sloshing around in it. Keeping my eyes on the floor, doing my best to ignore the penetrating stare Seraphina has glued on my face, my nostrils flare as I swallow a lump, and finally pull in enough air to inflate my lungs. Not letting me out of her sight until I've emptied the glass, the monster hasn't moved an inch away from me. The cloudiness in the liquid gives away her subtle way of keeping me docile. God only knows what she has put in it.

Not that I care, per se.

Every day when she brings the glass of water to me, I drink it with no complaint because it will stop the pain. She is a master of inflicting pain without placing a finger on you. The last time I refused to drink what she offered it felt like the skin was slowly melting off my bones. She chants and does crazy magic that hurts like hell. Magic, a thing from fairytales, is actually real.

A shiver rakes my spine.

"I don't have all day, girl. Get on with it." Folding her skinny arms over her chest, she glares down her nose at me.

Swallowing thickly once more, I press the warm rim of the glass to my lips and gulp it as fast as I can. Water trickles down on the sides of my face, soaking my chin and neck. Staring with unseeing eyes at the wall before me, I drink it all until there is nothing left. Not even Seraphina's gleeful chuckle can make me feel anything anymore.

I can't remember how long I've been here. It may be days, even years. She separated me from my two best friends, tricking us with a call for an audition. Once we were there, with her trap set, we had no way out. Now, I have nowhere to run, no one to turn to that can help me.

I've been at her mercy since.

She keeps asking me to play my violin, either for herself where she sits with her eyes closed and arms spread wide, or for groups of people that leer at me with hungry gazes. It's a never ending loop that leaves me barely standing on my feet after each performance. I call it a performance because she makes me dress up, do my make up, and look immaculate every time.

Even when she's my only audience.

Each note brings the golden thread of light that connects her chest to mine. That cursed night when she tied me to her pops to the front of my mind and steals my breath away.

"Excellent, Melody." Seraphina clapped louder, a wicked smile twisting her once-pretty face in a terrifying grimace. "I knew you had it in you."

"Where is everyone?" Still searching the empty church, I took a few steps back. "Vi! Harmony!"

Sound

Seraphina chuckled, the sound like nails on a chalk-board grating on my nerves. "Keep calling. They might answer."

"Where are my friends?" Snapping out of whatever is happening to my head, I glared at her. "What did you do to them?"

"Don't concern yourself with them." Cutting the air with her hand, she stalked towards me. "You, my dear, have bigger problems."

"Where are my friends?" Pushing the words through clenched teeth, I gripped my violin tighter. It'd break my heart to damage my instrument, but I would break it across her head if she was within reach.

"They are around, with problems of their own." Grinning like the cat that ate the canary, she moved closer. "You have no idea what you are, do you?"

"What are you talking about you, psycho?" Dread was like lead in my belly, the violin shaking in my sweaty trembling hand.

"You'll learn with time. But now that I have you, you will not escape from me." Seraphina lunged at me.

She was much faster than I expected. One second, she was a few yards away from the podium, the next she stood in front of me, her long nails digging in the skin of my neck where she gripped my throat. I struggled to free myself, but she pressed a spot that rendered me useless while making my hands hanging limply to my sides.

The violin dropped on the floor.

"Per me ego potestas penes universum mentis. Tuae aciem perstringere donum, ut serviant mihi," Seraphina chanted in Latin, and I had no idea how I understood the gibberish she spoke. "By the power vested in me, I bind your gift to serve me."

"What are you doing?"

Horrified, I watched when a bright, glowing cord, like a live electric wire, snaked out from her chest and attached to mine. I could feel it when it sank its claws deep inside my soul, the pain so excruciating stars danced in front of my eyes. Seraphina inched closer, her face only inches from mine. Her breath fanned my face. The last thing I remem-

bered before everything turned black were her pupils turning vertical and her eyes glowing bright orange. An explosion shattered everything, and the darkness enveloped me.

I startle when her icy cold fingers snatch the empty glass, knocking it against my lip and shaking off the memory. My teeth cut the inside of my lower lip, and the metallic taste of blood floods my mouth. The tip of my tongue traces the slight cut and I finally bring my focus back to the present. My gaze finds her face, a slight tightening of my belly the only emotion coursing through me when I see the smile stretching her red-painted lips plastered there.

"There you go," she coos at me, her hand gliding patronizingly over my hair in a mocking caress. "Doesn't that make you feel better?" Her cold, clammy fingers pinch my cheek like pincers. I barely stop myself from flinching. "You even have a bit of color back on your face. I will not have you looking like you're about to keel over on the stage tonight, you hear me?"

"Yes ma'am." When the words pass my numb lips, there is no inflection in my voice.

"Excellent!" I jump slightly when she claps her hands excitedly, the glass from a moment ago nowhere to be seen. "Now get ready. You look disgusting and you're up in thirty minutes. We have important guests tonight, so I will not have you embarrass me." With one last look that promises all sorts of pain if I don't do what she wants, she sweeps out of the room.

Blowing out a breath, my shoulders sag when the door locks with a soft click. Pressing both hands over my face, I scrub roughly over it a few times, burying the anger and helplessness threatening to drown me, as deep as I can. The drink she forced down my throat makes me sluggish, but it does not stop me from inwardly seething because of my situation. Defiance has proved ineffective and extremely painful. I'm stuck here no matter what I try, at least so far. Until I have a new plan, I will just have to play along with her. If she believes I've given up on the idea of escaping, maybe she'll make a mistake.

"Tough chance." Snorting humorously, I look around the sparse room. "The chances of Seraphina making a mistake are as good as seeing those blue eyes again."

A sharp ping stabs me at that thought and I rub at the center of my chest in hopes it will go away. My eyes landed on him what seems like a lifetime ago, I know it's foolish to keep thinking about the intriguing man. It was just a moment in time, two barely understood sentences in a club too loud to be able to think in, little less speak. I really am deplorable for obsessing over a guy that may have been asking where the bathroom is for all I know instead of trying to find a way out of here. Yet, I can't seem to get his face out of my mind.

It's one of the only things keeping me from falling apart in my prison: those soul-piercing blue eyes, the only other thing being the insane idea that I can escape. A girl can dream.

Lifting off the narrow bed I am perched on, I snatch the black corset that is sitting at the end of it. It takes a good ten minutes to wiggle my way into it, and even still, my ribcage protests from the tight, squeezing sensation, which of course pushes my breasts up for everyone to see. And that is another thing Seraphina enjoys: making me dress so out of my comfort zone that I feel rattled and unable to focus. The tight black leather pants and high-heeled ankle black boots are next, followed by the lacy elbow-length gloves. The rose patterns on the lace draw my gaze and I trace them with a fingertip. A sigh passes my pursed lips when I straighten, eyes locking on the violin waiting patiently on the only chair in this small, claustrophobic room.

Guilt almost chokes me because I know I'll enjoy every moment I'm able to play my instrument. I try to hate it, and I do my best to force myself to be miserable with every note I play, but it's always to no avail. I don't know what Seraphina is trying to achieve or do by keeping me here, but I know one thing for sure: because I love playing, I'm as guilty as she is for whatever she is doing.

Chapter Two

Étienne

"Any luck?"

Pausing in my stride, feet faltering at Lucien's voice, I unhurriedly turn and look at him. One shoulder leaning on the doorframe of his bedroom, his scrutinizing eyes search my face, and it's as if he can read my mind. I watch him, thinking I'll find anger or disappointment in his features—the same thing I'm feeling—but all I find is a stoic expression giving nothing away. Frustration claws at me, but I know it has nothing to do with my brother and everything to do with my inability to get us out of the mess we are in. Placing both hands in my pockets, I incline my head to him, inviting him to walk with me.

"I haven't made progress at all," I admit when he pushes off the door and falls in step beside me. "He is mindless by now; there is no way he is hiding something from me. Either he truly doesn't know who hired them, or ..."

My throat closes at the thought choking me with rage. "Or magic is involved and is silencing him."

Lucien says nothing for a while—a trait my middle brother does not possess on the best of days. It speaks volumes about the gravity of our situation. Ever since two weeks ago when we were attacked in front of a night club by a group of mercenaries—assassins from our kind hired to kill all three of us—we haven't learned anything useful. At first, we thought that the French court—the one my father ruled as a vampire king before he was killed—finally discovered us here in North America. We managed to stay under the radar for just over fifty years, but our luck was bound to run out eventually. To our surprise, the attack that night didn't come from the one who'd killed our father and wanted our own heads.

It took a damn cat turning our lives upside down to figure that out.

Even then, we were no closer to finding the truth. The only thing we learned was that magic was involved. Following the damn cat led us to an old church left in ruins on the outskirts of town, and it was drenched in enough magic to choke me. Of course, the beautiful music coming from within was like a siren's song, luring us forward as well. I still had no idea how we managed to resist it that night.

To this day, that is still all the information we have.

"You're growling," Lucien points out, his tone conversational as he keeps his gaze trained in front of him.

"J'ai envie de rugir, pas de grogner, mon frère." He snorts at my murmured confession that I want to roar instead of growl, because I spoke the truth.

"Est-ce que cela résoudra nos problèmes? Nous pouvons rugir ensemble si tel est le cas. " Flicking his eyes to my face, the humor in his words evaporates in the blink of an eye, his offer to roar with me all but forgotten. "I can try to persuade him to speak, even though I know you think I'll kill him if you leave me alone with him. Perhaps I'm rough, but I'm not stupid. I'm well aware how much we need that scum still breathing."

"I don't think roaring will solve our problems. Doing it alone, or together with you as you so kindly offered." Ignoring his request to question our prisoner on his own I answer Lucien's first question. "I do, however, believe that the girl is somehow connected with it all." My heart punches my ribcage with an audible thump, and my fists clench in the pockets of my pants. "The more I think about it, the more sense it makes."

"And you've been thinking about it quite a bit I can see," Lucien drawls as we reach my office.

Head snapping in his direction, my hand tightens on the doorknob, the metal groaning under my grip. Lucien lifts both hands in surrender, somehow managing to look as innocent as a virgin on her wedding night. Taking a step away from me, his eyes widen in mocking fear. I bare my teeth at him.

"About the connection … You've been thinking about the connection, I meant. No one said anything about the girl, definitely not me."

Forcing my fingers to release the doorknob one at a time, I straighten, my chin hitting my chest when I pinch the bridge of my nose between a thumb and forefinger. Not that his jab was far off the mark. Since it is *so* spot on, it makes me want to rip his throat out. Blowing a lungful of air out, I crack my neck to alleviate the tightness in the back of my skull. Killing my own brother will be monumentally stupid. As if hearing my thoughts, he sobers and stands straighter while he eyes me warily.

"I need a drink." Pushing the door open, I let the scent of leather, ink, and old parchment wash over me, calming my emotions. I haven't struggled with control like this in centuries.

"You and me both." Waiting until I'm halfway through the office, Lucien enters behind me before closing the door. "It might help with keeping my mouth shut when it needs to be." I raise an eyebrow at him as I lower myself in the chair. "Or maybe not." Grimacing, he beelines for the bar in the corner.

"There is something we are missing, it's mocking us and it's staring us in the face." Nodding when he lifts a bottle of whisky, I lean on the desk and watch him pour us both two fingers straight. "We've been here long enough that any other supernatural would've made their move long ago, if they were aware of us. Why now? What triggered this if it has nothing to do with home…or the girl?"

"And you are sure the girl is connected?" Placing the glass between my hands, he sits across from me. "It's not a jab. I've been trying to put it all together myself, although I must admit I haven't given the girl too much thought."

I search his face and he allows me, staring back at me unblinking. That's a very good question. I'm really not sure if she is connected, but everything in me says she is. If my gut feeling was not enough, the cat guiding my gaze to the violin with the broken bow laying next to it in the ruined church would've been a good nudge in the right direction the night we followed the cursed creature. My thoughts cloud over, the girl's features coming uninvited to the front of my mind, her tear-streaked face hauntingly beautiful.

My skin pebbles, shivers crawling over me like I've walked over a freshly dug grave. I lift the drink to hide my reaction from my brother.

"I can't see how a human can be connected," Lucien muses, noticing my distraction. "Apart from luring us to feed on her, what can a human girl do to one of us?"

Glass lifted hallway to my lips, I freeze, his words stabbing my brain and shattering the image of her in my head. My whole body stiffens, the barely-contained power's thread unraveling until it blasts around me like a tidal wave. The predator has lost control. Lucien jerks on his chair and the drink drops from his fingers, spilling over his lap. It takes great effort to pull myself back, and the glass in my hand groans as cracks spiderweb from my fingers.

"Was she human?" Lucien's glowing gaze locks on mine when I murmur the question. A line forms between his brows but his shoulders don't relax.

"What?"

"The girl." Lowering the drink to the desk, I release it slowly as not to break the glass and destroy the papers scattered on it. "Was she human?"

"Of course she was human." His scowl deepens and he pulls on his drenched pants with two fingers in disgust. "Look what you fucking made me do. Rain in your control before we announce to everyone where we are, will you? Apart from the three of us, everyone in that club was human. We would've known otherwise."

"I had no effect on her." Smirking at his glower, I lean back in the chair. "Neither did the two of you and we were standing right in front of her." This may explain why I can't get her out of my mind. I want to cry out in joy.

"She was hum—"

The door to the office bangs open and cuts off Lucien's protest, my youngest brother standing at the threshold with a huge grin plastered on his boyish face.

"J'ai dés Nouvelles." Grin widening, he saunters into the

office. "Get ready because we are going out," Moël announces, puffing out his chest.

"Everyone has gone insane in this fucking house," Lucien snaps, but I can't look away from the twinkle of excitement in Moël's eyes.

"You said you have news?" Watching him give Lucien a dismissive glance, I track my youngest brother until he stops at the corner of my desk.

"I think I found the girl." The intent look on Moël's face stops my heart, my ribs tightening so suddenly I'm left with no air in my lungs.

"Where?" I'm already off the chair rounding the desk. "Where is she?"

"As I said, we are going out." Reaching in the back pocket of his jeans, Moël pulls out three tickets and fans himself with them, his hair fluttering around his face like in a shampoo commercial the humans love to watch. "We got invited to a solo concert." His eyes bore into mine. "A violin solo."

My knees almost give out, so I place a hand on the desk to keep myself standing. He found the girl. Dread and excitement overwhelm me. Hopefully neither of my brothers noticed.

Chapter Three

Melody

The sound of hushed voices and the scraping of chairs reaches my ears as I inch along the dark hallway, tattering on the thin heels of my boots. Rubbing the tip of my nose with the back of my hand, I try to ignore the scent of damp soil, dust, and a sweet cloying stench that I can't name. I think it's the smell of magic since it clings to Seraphina every time she is near.

A snort escapes me at the thought.

I'm as batshit crazy as she is if I'm thinking about magic and what kind of smell it has. What's next? Vampires and werewolves fighting while fairies flap their wings around? Snickering at the image I slide my feet on the tiled floor, the heels catching between the tiny gaps. Deep down, I'm aware that I should be worried and scared—angry even— that I can't fight the bitch, but whatever she gives me to drink makes me feel mellow, almost like I'm in a drunk-like state.

Clutching the violin and bow in my sweaty palms, I wiggle restlessly in the corset, the wires pinching the skin at my sides painfully. Like a live doll that Seraphina is playing dress up with, here I am, a puppet with no strings to do her bidding. Not visible strings anyway. My throat tightens with too many emotions to name when I reach the juncture where the hallway opens to the wide area in Chalice, which is what Seraphina named the church she uses as a prison for us. Adrenaline spikes through my veins at the thought of Viola and Harmony.

I know I will see them tonight.

Seraphina's twisted mind thrives on making all of us suffer. Seeing each other across the room without being able to touch or talk is one of her torture techniques. She might think it's a punishment—and it was for a while—but to me, this is hope. I can see they are alive. As long as we're still breathing we can find a way out of here. At least that's what I tell myself so I don't drop on the ground and sob until I'm raw. I'm very good at ignoring the haunted looks in my friends eyes and the impossible situation we are in. If I face it, that bitch will win.

I won't let her win if it's the last thing I do.

"It's such a pleasure to see all of you here tonight." Seraphina's sweet, charming voice floats in the air and I gag at the fakeness in it. "Each and every single one of you gave up one precious thing for the opportunity to be here today. How does that make you feel?"

The blood curdles in my veins at her words. Poking my head out from around the corner, my gaze passes quickly over the people occupying every available space in the room. Faces glowing with excitement, wide eyes watching the bitch like she is a messiah preaching the words of whatever God they believe in, they roar their answers. Young and old, everyone has a manic look from the light of the candles twinkling in their eyes. My heart shrivels in my chest.

A girl around my age sits close to where I'm leaning around the corner. When she lifts her cup, she greedily gulps the contents. The glass isn't even placed on the table before she waves her fingers at the handful of people holding large trays with drinks perched precariously on them, balancing them on one hand. Zeroing in on the drinks, my fingers tighten on my violin. I have no doubt in this moment that Seraphina is giving these people the same thing she is giving me. But why?

I know it's her. Somehow, she is sucking out my energy while I play. These people don't play music. So what is it that she takes from them? Or is it like a drug they get hooked on so they keep coming for more? Shaking my head, I lean back and thump my head on the wall behind me. No, it can't be that. The people that get invited here are never the same. A headache stabs me in the back of the eyes and blurs my vision. Seraphina's voice brings me out of my turbulent thoughts.

"Tonight I have a treat for you." She makes a dramatic pause to build the anticipation in the room. "Our young violinist will play just for you, the beautiful Partita No. 2 in D minor by Bach. Not one eye will stay dry in this place before the night ends. Are you ready?" She stretches both arms to the side, as if hugging the place, while the crowd hoots in excitement.

Cold sweat trickles down my back and my heart gallops wildly against my ribs. One spotlight comes to life, the blinding light falling on the only chair on the stage, which is erected in the middle of the wide space. I feel the tug at the center of my chest making my feet move on their own to pull me out of my hiding spot. Seraphina's cold, hungry gaze finds me immediately, and a blast of arctic chill spreads through my bones. That's exactly how she looks ... hungry.

A hush falls over the room, the clicking of my heels on the tiles echoing like gunshots and bouncing off the walls and high ceilings. Everything in me screams to turn around and run away to safety, yet I move more gracefully than ever before as I make my way to her outstretched arms. She hugs me like a mother would a child, her gesture earning her the sighs from the audience she expected. Goosebumps pinch my skin where she touches me and I grind my teeth, unable to say a word. Fingers squeezing so hard my nails dig into my skin, she tilts her chin to one side of the room, then the other. My gaze follows her direction and a lump forms in my throat when I see Viola on one side, Harmony on the other.

My friends watch me with parted lips, their eyes too wide on their pale faces. I haven't seen them since last time she made me dress up to play. The dark circles under their eyes are the same ones I see in the mirror before I cover them with the makeup Seraphina supplies. It's like putting on a new skin, enough to fool anyone into thinking I am as healthy as a glowing red apple, but no one can see the worms eating you inside. Do my friends think I'm better off than them by seeing me all made up? The terror in their eyes tells me no, tells me they can see through this mask. They know I'm just as bad as they are.

I lose sight of both of them when Seraphina jerks on my arm and forces me to sit on the lone chair. With a barely there touch on my hair, she drifts away and leaves me staring at the violin in my hands. I want to rebel. I want to jump up and smash the instrument at my feet into pieces and scream from the top of my lungs for all of them to run.

Sound

The violin swings gracefully in my hand, my chin lowering gently on the rest to hold it in place. The bow comes next, hovering above the strings as I squeeze my eyes tightly shut.

The first note is a dagger in my chest.

Such a beautiful piece of music by Bach is sublimely satisfying when you hear it in its original form. A single violin, no matter how good the musician is, is only able to hint at the vast implications of it. A good performance, like the one I forcefully offer, may be taken as the best guide to interpretation on the organ the composer favored so much, yet it's still unable to encompass it fully.

I hate it that I'm enjoying it so much, but I can't stop myself. It speaks to something inside me, even while I feel my strength trickling down, the golden cord snaking from my chest glittering in the spotlight. My arm feels heavy where I hold the bow sawing at the strings without a moment of a pause. The notes rise and fall until I can barely summon enough strength to suck in tiny sips of air.

The music stops.

My head hangs low on my neck, tears soaking my cheeks and plopping against the back of my hands, which are folded in my lap. I hear the murmurs of people leaving, the shuffling of their feet fading away. Silence presses on my shoulders so thick I don't know how I'm still able to sit on the chair. With great effort, I lift my head and my heart stops.

Blue eyes—ones I know too well because they haunt my every dream—lock on mine from across the empty room. Confusion and rage twist the handsome face that has no right to exist in this world. No one is that perfect. No one. My heart kicks up painfully in my chest when he takes a step toward me, coming out of the shadows that were covering him. Lips parting, the scream for help lodges in my throat when I hear Seraphina hiss from behind me like a feral animal. Her nails rip the skin of my shoulder when she yanks me back, the chair falling along with my body. The violin I am clutching for dear life drops from my numb fingers only to clatter on the floor.

"Please ..." is all that can pass my unmoving lips as the world disappears around me.

The last thing I see before darkness takes me is the beautiful man sprinting in my direction with determination stamped on his face.

But he is too late.

Chapter Four

Étienne

"I detest magic." Unlike my two brothers, I hate the vile thing.

Lucien grins at me as if I told him a joke while we watch humans trickle inside the abandoned church. What used to be a pile of ruins—which we saw with our own eyes the night we followed the damn cat—is now a brand-new building staring me in the face with doors wide open. I was being serious when I said I detested magic a few moments ago. The three of us are acutely aware of it, more so than anyone else of our kind. More so than my father was. Nothing good can come out of something that can trap you, or worse, trap your mind.

Centuries ago, witches and vampires worked well together as allies. Until one magic user decided to test a theory about draining a vampire to achieve immortality without being dependent on blood. The records of it are lost and no one knows if it has ever been achieved or not.

But since then, we do know we are mortal enemies. I will sooner rip the throat out of a witch than an assassin hell bent on killing me.

A shiver rattles my bones.

"Shall we—"

"Not yet," cutting off Lucien, my eyes narrow at the church.

The wards erected around the place shimmer before my eyes like a cobweb catching light. The spell is a complicated one crisscrossing over the dome, too many triggers flashing through it as if daring me to try my luck. Unassuming humans push through, the magic like ghostly fingers clinging to their clothing and hairs, solidifying my theory that they are unfit to survive in this world. Regardless of being unaware of anyone else existing aside from them, they are willing prey. I can't even blame the magic user for luring them in.

"What are we waiting on?" Lucien grumbles from my right. "An invitation? We have three; let's go."

"Do you not see?" Fists clenching at my sides, I search for a loophole, a way to trick the wards or break them apart.

I get nothing.

"I see the wards." Snarling at me, I can feel his scowl on the side of my head. "I also see there is no way of sneaking past them. So fuck it, let's just storm inside and rip it apart."

"And then what?" Turning to face him, I let him squirm under my glare. "End up trapped in the wards until the sun comes up or alerting the witch so it flees and we can't find them?"

"I don't have time to sit around and wait." Spitting the words out, he drops his gaze wisely.

"Something else is more important than staying alive, brother?" Looking down my nose at him, I wait for an explanation but only get a muscle twitching in his cheek. "I didn't think so."

"C'est le piège parfait." Moël's soft murmur comes from behind my back.

Keeping my stern gaze locked on Lucien for a moment longer, I finally face my youngest brother. The comment is spot on. This is a perfect trap. His youthful face is solemn, a line bunching his forehead and making him resemble me more than ever before. The ready smile and easygoing character always makes him look younger than the two of us. Not at this moment. The gravity of that presses on my chest like a mountain. Moël is not one to worry too much. That's my job to overthink things and ponder them to death. He removes whatever is supposed to concern him by tilting his lips up and smiling.

"Any idea on how to go through without being noticed?" I can hear Lucien grinding his teeth over the sound of my voice.

"I have an idea, but I'm not sure I like it much." Jerking his chin up, he looks to the side of the church.

Following the direction of his gaze, I can't stop the growl that vibrates my chest. The damn black cat sits smugly just outside the wards, tail flicking lazily behind it. With its penetrating glare, it sees us where we hide in the shadows—the ones that are part of our predatory abilities—as if there's nothing hindering its vision. No one can penetrate the mist—not even me.

"You think it can see us?" Abandoning his shitty attitude, Lucien steps closer to us.

"It's been following my movements without missing a beat if that answers your question." Moël's frown deepens.

My mouth opens, the words dying on my tongue when a haunting melody reaches my ears. Ribs tightening, the air is forced out of my lungs with a whoosh. I see both my brothers stiffen on either side of me but I don't dare move. Frozen where I stand, I'm not sure how long I listen to it, and I realize too late that I'm rubbing at the center of my chest with a clenched fist. Focusing on the cat, I see the creature also swaying to the notes that are drifting in the air. That's when I notice it.

The silence.

Every other sound is gone, the quiet suffocating and thundering in my ears louder than any noise could ever be. For a moment, I even think life is holding its breath so it can hear the heart-wrenching beauty of the song being played. Everything disappears, even the soft inhale and exhale of our breaths. Everything but the notes floating around us. Panic grips me when the sound slows and the melody reaches its end.

The cat locks its orange gaze on mine, flashing in defiance. Whatever has been holding me in place releases my limbs. The creature darts to the side and I bolt after it. I can hear my brothers behind me but I neither stop nor think. Rounding the building, the cat waits there for me. A moment ticks by before it lifts its tale as if daring me to follow, then it disappears inside the church.

"Étienne, wait."

Lucien's shout comes a second too late. I follow the creature, bracing for impact when a solid brick wall comes into view. I'm running too fast to be able to stop the impact so instead I let instinct take over, lifting my arm and crossing it in front of my face to protect my head. My skin burns where the wards touch it and I stumble, almost falling on my face when I meet no resistance.

My gaze locks on dark, sad eyes and a tear-stained face.

The girl sits slumped in a chair and is barely keeping her

Sound

head up with a glaring spotlight shining over her. Her gaze locks on mine and my heart stops beating from her desperate look. Anger battles confusion until her lips part, and I lean forward as desperate as she is to hear what she says. A bony hand comes from the shadows behind her, red painted nails tearing the skin on her shoulder. Dark red blood drips over her milky skin before she whispers.

"Please ..."

Launching forward with everything in me, my hand stretches out and pain tears at my shoulder as I try to grab her. The chair flips over, pulling her along with it. Shadows swallow her, the spotlight shining from above not reaching them. The violin falls on the floor with a loud thump just as I reach the spot where she used to be.

An empty chair tipped over with legs sticking accusingly at me is the only thing there. Keeping eye on everything around me, I snatch the instrument off the ground. It's still warm where her hand was holding it, the bottom part wet from her tears. Another shiver passes over me when the wards disappear, and I find myself in the same ruins I know too well. Heck, they were why I found this church in the first plate.

My fingers tighten on the violin. "Je te trouverai." A promise or a threat, I'm not sure, but the vow in my voice stuns me. "I will find you."

Chapter Five

Melody

With a groan, I roll on my side. The hard-as-a-rock mattress hurts my bones, the spring poking and digging into my skin. A pounding headache with its own heartbeat thumps behind my closed lids and in my temples. Breathing through my nose, I hold my breath hoping not to vomit.

"I'm never drinking again." Panting when the bile rises in the back of my throat, I push up and swing my legs off the bed.

A wet nose bumps the back of my hand, a furry head rubbing against me soon after. Keeping my eyes closed, I trail my fingers over the purring friend that has woken me up, scratching it behind one ear.

"You are being mean for waking me up, Salmon." I chuckle when he hisses at the name I gave him, regretting it the same second. "Karma, my friend, is a bitch. I think this is payback for naming you after a fish."

Sound

If a cat can meow in approval, Salmon definite does this.

Cracking one eyelid open, I squint at him. He found me in this room the first night I was trapped in this place. Since then, he is the only one that keeps me company, that is unless Seraphina comes with her drugs and demands. I have no idea how the cat gets inside the room when the door is locked, but I refuse to think he's just a figment of my imagination because I'm slowly going crazy here.

I can't have imaginary friends, can I?

Eyeing the cat, fast as a snake I snatch his tail and tug on it. Hissing, he swipes at me with sharp claws and tears three lines in the skin of my forearm. Blood, gathers at the scratches and the stinging, burning pain brings tears to my eyes. Not because it hurts. No, these are tears of joy.

"I'm sorry, Salmon." Sniffing pathetically, I coerce him to come closer by wiggling my fingers, which he knows is a promise for a scratch. His eyes narrow but he slinks towards me. "I need to make sure you're real. Otherwise, it means I'm losing my mind and that won't be good for anyone. Especially me."

My belly tightens when he gives me a look of pity. Can a cat give you a pitiful look? My brain rattles just attempting to think, so I push the thought aside.

"Last night was a rough one," I tell my very-real and not-at-all-imaginary cat visitor. "She usually drains me a lot every time I play the violin but never to a point where my blood is too sluggish to move through my veins."

The skin on my arms prickles with goosebumps at the intent look the cat gives me. If I don't know better, I may think it understands everything I say. Shaking off the unease, I continue scratching the spot he loves and his purring increases in volume, filling up the quiet room.

Keeping my breathing even and slow, I glance around the tiny space.

"How do you come in here, huh?" Gliding my hand over his back, I feel every ridge of his spine when he hunches up in an arch. "I'm pretty sure bitch face would've stopped you from keeping me company if she knew you could do that."

I can't stop the giggle when he gives me a smug look, as if saying, "Girl, you have no idea how smart I am. I'll never get caught." When I realize what I'm doing, I choke on a laugh. I don't want to go nuts in this place. I will not talk to cats.

The rustling of fabric behind the closed door makes my heart lodge in my throat. I freeze like a deer caught in headlights as I stare at the door wide-eyed. Luckily, Salmon does not suffer from stupidity. One second, my hand is pressing on his back, and the next he is bolting behind the vanity holding the large mirror to the wall.

I blink.

There is no space there for a larger-than-your-average cat to fit. A mouse can't even squeeze there, and I know because I left nothing unturned the first night she locked me in this room. A frown tightens my forehead right before the door swings open and I forget all about the cat and impossible spaces.

Seraphina sashays into my room. "You are awake." I shrink back when she glares at me with hatred. "Good."

Her skin is glowing in the low-hanging light, a pink hue on her cheeks giving her a youthful appearance unlike the first time I saw her. I thought she was middle aged then, but every time she comes she looks more and more my age. I'm only twenty-two. Noticing me staring at her, she grins with no humor.

Sound

"I look good, don't I?" Spinning in place, the black dress that hugs her curves swirls around her bare feet, the blonde curls floating around her face. "I feel amazing."

"That must be nice." As soon as the words are out, I bite my tongue and taste blood. There's no way she misses the snide tone. The scowl replacing her smile confirms it.

Stupid, Melody. You are so foolish for not keeping your mouth shut. Berating myself internally, I blink innocently at her as if I meant the words in a nice way.

She doesn't buy what I'm trying to sell.

Snatching my arm, she yanks me up and off the bed. The world tilts on its axis, my stomach giving a hard lurch. I press my lips tight so I don't puke all over her, although seeing that may be worth it. I laugh hysterically through meshed-up lips.

"Something funny, girl?" Shaking me like a dog shakes a bone, she sneers in my face.

Lips parting, Seraphina takes a breath. I steel myself, preparing for insults or pain to come, but she stops and frowning. Her head turns slowly to look around the room and I'm not sure how long I can hold the bile back. Fear sinks sharp claws in my lungs, raking over them and sucking the air out.

"No one has been in this room?" Since it's a question, I shake my head frantically because I'm unable to speak.

"No way she found out what she is or what she can do." Murmuring under her breath, she catches herself and closes her mouth with an audible snap.

I'm more confused now than ever before.

With a disgusted look, she throws me back on the bed—the woman is much stronger than she looks—and stalks around the small space like a caged tiger. I've seen one pissed off in a circus once when I was young. That wild beast can't hold a candle to the two-legged one prowling in front of me in this moment. Seraphina halts, her gaze honing-in on me.

"You think I didn't see him there?" Dumbfounded, all I can do is blink like a simpleton at her words. "You think one of his kind can save you?"

Knowing better than to not answer when she asks a question, I whisper a word through numb lips. "No."

"Damn right he won't." A leer twists her face, and the blood stops circulating through my body at the sight. "I will suck him dry just like you if I see him sniffing around here again, do you understand?"

My heads nods jerkily. I can't speak to save my life right now. A menacing smile pulls her red lips up, making all sorts of alarms blare in my head. The bedframe rattles, the metal headboard thumping on the wall from how hard my body is shaking. Seraphina's hand lifts between us, her long fingers curling like she is gripping the air in the palm of her hand. Searing pain blooms inside me, my ears buzzing like a cloud of bees has invaded my brain. My back bows, my mouth gaping open in a silent scream. It's all consuming pain that melts my bones. I can't even whimper.

"I own your pathetic life." Coming closer, she stares down at me. "I will take it if I feel like it, and you better remember that." Her hands drop to her side and the pain stops.

It's so sudden that I have no time to control my body's reaction. Hunching forward, I get as far as the edge of the bed before vomiting all over the bottom of her dress and her bare feet. Sucking in shuddering breaths, I don't dare look up. All my muscles lock as I wait for the punishment to come. To my surprise, she laughs.

The bitch laughs at me.

Sound

Rage burns like an inferno inside me.

"You are pathetic." Chortling happily, she spins on her heel and stalks out, locking the door behind her.

I hang off the bed, angry tears dropping down my face while my hair is like a curtain pooling on the floor. A wet nose bumps on my white-knuckled grip on the bed. Sniffing, I tilt my head to the side and see Salmon through the curling strands.

'It's okay, buddy." Hiccupping, I pull another shuttering breath into my lungs. "It didn't even hurt that much this time."

Salmon gives me a sad meow, and I know he doesn't buy the lies I'm trying to sell him either.

Chapter Six

Étienne

Shifting restlessly from one foot to the other, I scan the area for the hundredth time. Leaving my brothers behind might not be the brightest of ideas but staying put isn't an option, the need to be here too strong for me to resist. It has to be magic conjuring me forward—at least that is what I tell myself as I lurk in the shadows like a feral beast. The heir to the French court stalking a human girl in a ruined church while waiting for a cat to show up as if I'm meeting an informant ... Yeah, I'll be a laughing stock for centuries to come.

I'll laugh at myself too.

"Je suis tellement idiot!" Calling myself an idiot is not the worst insult that comes to mind.

Pushing off the tree I'm leaning on, my shoulders turn but my gaze stays locked on the abandoned place. Reluctantly, I lean back on the trunk, folding my arms over my chest. I stood here so long already that another few minutes won't make a difference. Still, my feet won't move.

Is she there now? Can she see through the illusion cast over the damn place? Is she laughing at how pathetic I look, like I'm some love-sick puppy unable to tear my eyes from the place? Anger clouds my thoughts and I almost miss the movement at the side of the church.

The hard punch of my heart against my breastbone is not missed by the cat staring at me from across the street. Its head cocks to the side, its tail swishing in agitation. My fangs throb in answer to its aggressive movements. We face each other for a long moment before it turns and disappears.

I'm across the street before the thought to move registers in my brain. Following just the end of the thick tail, I round the corner and skid to a stop before I find the cat not even a foot away from me. It has never allowed any of us this close. I freeze so I don't spook it. Maybe I can grab it if I lure it into a false sense of safety.

As if reading my thoughts, the damn cat darts further away.

Glancing around to make sure no one will witness my embarrassment, I crouch down to bring myself closer to its level. Feeling all types of idiotic, I swallow a growl and take a deep breath. The damn creature leans eagerly forward as if in anticipation. I frown at the reaction and it jerks back, acting as innocent as a shark waiting to bite your head off.

"Are you a friend or a foe?" It looks at me like I'm a simpleton, tail flicking mockingly behind it. I cannot find the means to disagree with it. "This was a very dumb idea."

Snarling at my stupidity, I start to climb to my feet, but the cat darts next to me and bumps its head where my hand is gripping my knee before retreating out of reach. Pausing,

I eye it suspiciously. It looks back at me with a sense of expectancy.

"Do you know the girl that plays the violin?" Its unblinking stare is my only answer. "Do you belong to the girl that plays the violin?" Rephrasing my question in hopes of a reaction, I get one.

My body lurches and I almost land on my ass. The cat hisses at me, sounding more feral than any beast I've ever heard. Laughter shakes my shoulders but I cough to cover it up when its hackles rise and its tail flicks faster in anger, ears pinned to the back of its head.

"Okay, okay." Lifting both palms up in surrender, I fight the smile lifting my lips. "No one owns you, I get it. We share the same sentiment on that front."

The cat's orange eyes narrow at me like it doesn't trust my words. This night is by far the craziest one I've had in my life. In my very long life since I'm a vampire.

Shaking the head to clear it, I sigh. "You helped me get through the wards so I could see the girl." Pausing, I watch for a reaction and I'm stunned when the cat nods its head slowly. "You are here with me because I'm alone." The realization hits me like a ton of bricks.

The cat nods again, eyeing me warily.

I'll think about why it doesn't want my brothers around later. Pushing my senses wide, I check for anyone sneaking in behind my back, but the coast is clear. Just me and the cat facing each other under the crescent moon. I watch the creature in contemplation. There is no way for me to know if it's telling the truth, but deep down I feel that it is. For some crazy reason, I'm crouched in the dirt next to an abandoned church talking to a cat. It's a good thing I am here in America.

I'm unfit to rule my kind, bloodlines be damned.

Sound

"Is the girl trying to trick me? Is she luring me here?" Voicing my fears, I'm taken aback by another angry hiss, the cat baring its pointy teeth at my face.

A knot loosens in my chest at the reaction.

"Is she in trouble? Is that way you've been trying to guide us here?" Choosing my words wisely, I stare at the cat.

It watches me for a long time, and just when I think I need to ask a different question, its head lowers in a slow nod.

There is not enough air on this street to inflate my lungs. The cat creeps further away and I realize a deep growl is rumbling in my chest. Swallowing the sound, I breathe through my nose, my nostrils flaring. The desperate look on her tear-streaked face is like a punch to my chest. It almost doubles me over.

I'm not sure why I care. I haven't cared about anything apart from finding a way to go back home in a very long time. But I can't find it in me to walk away. Everything else be damned. I'm going to get to the bottom of this. But before I dive in head-first against magic and witches, I have to know one crucial thing that's been bothering me from the moment I set eyes on her.

"Is she human?" Holding my breath, I watch the cat like a hawk. My answer is a flick of a tail and an unblinking stare boring into my eyes.

"I knew she couldn't be human." Having it confirmed—even by a cat—is enough to build an urgency in my gut. "Okay, I'm ready when you are. Lead the way."

Chapter Seven

Melody

"I don't think the bitch needs anything else to kill me." Huffing in annoyance, I roll my head while staring at the walls. "I'll die of boredom in a week."

Scratching absently at my ribs where the wires of the corset left bruises, I'm scared to close my eyes. Since the day I was trapped here, nobody has ever stayed after the music stops.

Until last night.

Does that mean he can come and go at will? How? More importantly, how did he find me? The questions swirling through my mind make me dizzy. This has to be a coincidence. What are the odds that I meet this guy a day before I'm brought here to be trapped in a nightmare? Seraphina's murmured words pop into my head. *"No way she found out what she is, or what she can do."*

What does that even mean?

It has everything to do with my music, that much I

know. The night the three of us played at the annual concert and people died, I knew something was wrong. As much as I'd love to place the blame on someone else, or believe the tabloids about a chemical terrorist attack, I can't. People died looking like dug out mummies from an archeologist's dream. One moment they were dancing, and the next they dropped like flies while I was buzzing with so much energy my skin felt too tight to contain me. So I can't find it in me to place it at someone else's feet. We did that.

I did that. But how?

There are too many why's and how's for my mushy brain to piece together right now. Being locked in this room, though, I don't have anything better to do. Even Salmon left me, too bored with my miserable mood. Not that I blame the cat. Leaving me doesn't sound like such a bad idea right now.

Sighing, I roll on my stomach and fold my arms to cushion my head. Bones protesting at the movement, I wiggle around until I'm kind of comfortable—if laying on a rock can be considered that. Seraphina usually brings the damn poison she makes me drink after I play but she skipped it today. She was either too high on whatever she takes from me, or the guy pissed her off.

A smile stretches my lips.

They may be working together or against each other, but I don't care. Anyone that pisses her off is good in my book. If pain doesn't follow, I will piss her off every chance I get. It's the little things that matter when your life goes to shit, and boy has mine gone haywire. I thought dealing with my depressed, always unhappy, and critical mother was a bad life. It gave me enough issues for a lifetime of therapy—if I ever decide to deal with it. I'm a psychologist's dream. Seraphina has shown me how wrong

I've been because that life was wonderful compared to this one.

A shuffle and a scrape against the wall behind the mirror jerks my head up. Staring intently at it for a while and holding my breath, I see nothing. Snorting at my excitement, I put my cheek down and press it on my arms. I think Salmon is coming back. Talking to a cat is better than talking to myself, or thinking.

Something darts into the room.

With a shriek, I bolt upright, banging my head on the wall at my back. My teeth rattle and stars dance in front of my eyes from the impact. Pressing a hand to keep my heart inside my chest, hysterical laughter bubbles up. The kicking of my heartbeat moves my arm, and it's too painful to be ignored. Panting, I scowl at Salmon, who is eyeing me like I'm an idiot while he licks his paw.

"That was not nice." My voice stutters, matching the galloping in my ribcage. "You gave me a heart attack."

If a cat can raise his eyebrow, I'm pretty sure Salmon does. Either way, he somehow manages to make me feel dumb. Pausing with his paw lowered in front of his face, he gives me a pointed look before resuming his grooming.

"Leave it to a cat to be an asshole." Blowing out a breath, I plop down on the bed. "No scratches for you at all today."

Something rattles behind the wall and the mirror shifts just enough to curdle my blood. My gaze flicks from it to Salmon, assuring myself that I'm actually seeing the cat inside the room. Cold sweat dampens my palms.

"Did you hear that?" Whispering because I'm too afraid to speak louder, I crawl off the bed.

Another scrape sounds and this time the vanity rattles from the hard thud against the wall, causing all the makeup to fall haphazardly on it (I might've turned OCD while here and arranged them by height and in groups). Feeling cold all over, my skin prickles with goosebumps as I stare at the wall like it'll come to life and attack me. Salmon, on the other hand, doesn't have my issues. He continues going to town on his paw, licking away like there is no tomorrow.

I glare at him.

Aren't cats supposed to be skittish and bolt at sudden noises? Turning away from the weirdo, I look around the room not sure what it is I'm looking for. A weapon? Can you defend yourself against something by brandishing mascara? I guess I can poke their eye out with it, because God knows I've done it enough times to myself and it hurts like the dickens. Taking a step to do just that, I see the lump from the corner of my eye next to the chair and I want to cry in relief. As fast as I can, I snatch one of the high-heeled boots I kicked off after Seraphina left this morning.

Retreating until the back of my knees bump against the bed, I clutch the boot to my chest. Cold sweat trickles down my back and tremors claw at my spine. Salmon is not exactly your typical cat, and since this is a nightmare, I don't know what other monsters can come inside this room. Considering everyone else seems to waltz right in whenever they choose, I guess it's been made to keep me in.

Soft murmurs reach my ears and get louder by the second. I'm either insane or someone is getting closer, and by the sounds coming my way, they are cursing up a storm under their breath. I don't understand the words they are speaking, though. It has to be a different language, or perhaps the thundering of blood in my ears is preventing it. I only know one thing for sure: someone is coming, and it's a man.

Mind spinning and fear bringing all sorts of scenarios to

my mind, I squeeze the boot so tight the heel almost digs a hole in my chest. Has Seraphina decided to start bringing men in this room? Is my music no longer enough for her? Will she now pimp me out to anyone who wants me? All the blood drains from my body at the thought, and a numbness like a tidal wave spreads through my neck and skull. Dark spots dance at the corners of my eyes and I'm hyperventilating. With one last hiss, a man walks through the wall.

Through the fucking wall.

"You." I'm not sure if I speak out loud or I just think the word.

Blue eyes widen in surprise, and Salmon releases a smug meow from beside me. Frozen in place, there is only one thing screaming like a siren in my head: *It's him. It's the guy from the club. He found me.* With that last internal shout, I do what every stupid girl does in all the low-budget horror movies.

I faint.

And it's really not one of my finest moments.

Chapter Eight

Étienne

This is what I get for following a supernatural cat through magic-infested grounds. Cursing up a storm, I cringe from the dust and cobwebs that cling to my skin and clothing while trudging through the darkness. Even with my sight I can't penetrate the pitch black, which tells me this is not an ordinary tunnel. It's a passage through the wards, a loophole—probably the very one I've been searching for. The top of my head brushes against the ceiling and something sticks to it. I shudder. If only Lucien could see me now, he'd have a field day teasing me. As if cleanliness and appreciation of the fine things in life is a crime or something.

The tip of my shoe hits a dip in the ground and pitches me forward. Stumbling, more curses hiss from my lips as my arm shoots out to catch myself before I fall into whatever covers this floor. No matter what it may be, I'm just glad I can't see it because the squishing sound my feet make is enough to raise all the hairs on my body. Grinding my teeth,

I pull my hand back from where presses against a moss-covered stone. At least I make myself think it's moss because otherwise I may not keep going. Wiping my palms on my pants, I continue forward, my lips twisting in aversion.

A distant, high-pitched sound penetrates the darkness from up ahead, but it's too low for me to hear it if comes from a male or female. Moving faster, I can't stop the onslaught of choice words that probably make my father turn in his grave.

"I'm going to skin that damn cat and string it up by its tail." Grinding the words through clenched teeth, I push further into the tunnel.

Reaching an area where the air is so dense I have to force my way through it, I call up my mist and wrap it around me like a cloak. It makes it easier to pass but not by much. Something whispers at the center of my chest, just a gentle, hesitant brush of energy that's gone too fast for me to examine it closely. Shaking off the feeling and releasing the mist, I ram through the tunnel with everything I've got.

Bursting out of the darkness, the dim yellow light makes me squint. The next moment, my gaze connects with wide, dark eyes on a pale-as-a-ghost face and I barely stop myself from gawking. The girl—the one with the violin—is standing across the room, her back pressed to the wall behind her as if she's trying to meld with it and disappear. She is hugging something to her chest, but I can't see it since I can't tear my gaze from her face. Dark circles spread like smudges under her eyes, accentuating her pale skin. Her full lips are parted in shock, but even with all that, she is still the most beautiful creature I have ever seen.

"You." The word is just a breath wrenched from her chest, but it reaches my ears as if it's a shout.

My heart thunders against my breastbone, my chest

Sound

getting too tight to allow oxygen into my lungs. I stand frozen, my legs like lead glued to the ground as I continue to stare at her. All thoughts flee my head, leaving it an empty desert with strong winds deafeningly echoing in my ears. Her soul-piercing eyes roll to the back of her head and she goes limp, crumpling on the floor.

I have never moved as fast as I do in this moment.

The back of my hand takes the impact where I hold her head in my palm. My other arm snakes around her narrow waist to pull her to my chest. She looks like a porcelain doll, small and fragile in my arms. Long, dark lashes cover the circles under her eyes, which are closed and unmoving. I want her to open them, to look at me more than I've wanted anything else in centuries. Soft breaths puff out from her parted lips, which calms the urge to destroy things that clamors inside me. With great effort, I lift my head and let my gaze turn from her face to the room.

The room is small, as big as the linen closet we have in the house. Stained walls press around me on all sides, a tiny bed no more than a pallet pushed to my left and a small desk with a tall mirror resting against the wall I used as an entrance. Black clothing is folded neatly at the edge of the mattress, and one stylish boot with a thin high heel is lying next to the only chair. A gray wooden door is next to where I'm kneeling while hugging the girl to me like someone might snatch her. The cat squats at the center of it all looking smugger than my brother Lucien when he is right about something, which is rare.

Warmth spreads through me like what I imagine the rays of the sun may feel like, though it is a pleasure I've never known. Nonetheless, the feeling startles me, so I lower my gaze to the girl in my arms. My eyes lock on hers where she watches me, the whites overtaking the dark color of her irises. The moment our gazes meet, my heart gives a hard lurch.

"Hello," her soft voice rasps before she clears her throat and swallows thickly. She doesn't move or try to get away, which makes the beast in me roar in approval, and the shock that courses through me at this renders me mute. "Who are you?" The sound passing her lips is more beautiful to my ears than the music she plays.

"Parle encore ma petite, j'aime le son de ta voix." Murmuring to her, I search her face, my chest rising and falling faster the longer I hold her in my arms.

"I have no clue what you just said in European, but it sounded beautiful." She bites her lip as soon as the words are out, her cheeks pinking in the process. I gawk like a fool. "I mean, I know European is not a language because Vi actually told me that. Not that I didn't know it before she pointed it out. By the sound of the rolling "R" in your accent it's French, right? Of course it's French. No one else speaks like they want to melt your panties off with just words." Sucking in a lungful of air, her cheeks get a little redder with every word she speaks, and that makes the edges of my lips twitch. "Apart from Spanish. That language can also melt your panties. Oh my God, I'm blabbering like a moron but I can't stop myself. I have no idea why I'm talking to you about melting panties. Please tell me you don't speak English. Or just kill me now. That's an option on the table too, just so you know." Groaning, she lifts her arms and covers her face with her hands.

"Si belle. Une telle innocence …" I want to remove her hands so I can keep looking at her but I don't want to let her out of my arms.

"You don't speak English." She peeks at me through her fingers warily, the words muffled from the hands. "Of course, you don't. Out of all the hot girls drooling over you in the club you came to talk to me." Lowering her hands and letting me see her face, she blows out a breath. "You probably thought I was working there, huh, and you wanted to ask where the bathroom was? I should've known the second a hottie like you acknowledged me."

I drink her in, searching her eyes for something I cannot name. Well aware I should help her up and release her, I can't find it in me to remove my arms from her body. If it lasts longer, I have a nagging feeling they'll have to pry her out of my dead hands. I must be staring at her for too long, or maybe I just look like an idiot because she offers me a too-bright smile, which confuses the hell out of me. And that's when it hits me. Everything she said washes over me, as well as the fact I have been speaking to her in my own language.

"I said, 'speak again little one, I love the sound of your voice.'" One side of my mouth lifts slightly when her eyes widen comically. My fingers move in her hair, the silky strands gliding over my skin. "And then I said, 'so beautiful, such innocence.'" She gawks with her mouth hanging open. My smile grows. "That night I wanted to learn your name. I was most definitely not looking for the bathroom ... Melody." She shivers at the sound of her name on my lips. So do I.

With an outraged shriek, her legs jackknife and she kicks me in the groin. My eyes cross and I release her as I hunch over in pain. Her small hands shove hard against my chest, catching me off guard and sending me on my ass where I cough pathetically with my hands clutching my bruised balls.

I knew I should've released her sooner.

Chapter Nine

Melody

"How do you know my name?"

Guilt jabs me in the chest when I see him rocking with both hands pressed between his thighs. His face looks like a tomato, scrunched up in agony. Nails digging in the wall behind me, I feel horrible for kneeing him in the junk. Not that I do it on purpose. At first, I think I am dreaming. God knows I dream about him enough, so I let myself stammer on like an idiot. When I realize he is real, embarrassment attacks me, especially when I realize he understands every stupid word falling from my mouth. At that point, all I want is to get away and hide.

I wince when a low groan comes from him.

It pisses me off that I have no clue who this guys is, how he got here, or why he is here. Still, I can't help but admire the way the muscles bunch on his arms and back with each movement he makes. And who looks hot as hell with a red, scrunched-up face? This guy apparently. I want to kick him again on this principle alone. He should look horrible, not hot.

"Your friend." The words are hissed through clenched teeth as the guy lifts on his knees.

"Huh?" Inching away, I press harder against the wall and frown at him.

"Your friend ..." Blowing out a breath, he straightens to his full height. I crane my head to keep eye contact and slam it into the wall. "She called you by your name before you ran away that night." How tall is this guy? Jesus, I'll need a brace if I keep staring up.

"You heard that?" Deciding I don't want to look like a child staring at a parent, I slide down the wall to put a little space between us. There, that's better.

"I did, yes." The tilt of his kissable lips sends my stomach somersaulting.

No! Not kissable lips. Bad, Melody. The guy is a creep that walks through walls, remember? Berating myself, I miss what he says next. Luckily, I can't look away from his *not* kissable lips so I see them moving.

"I'm sorry, what?" Pinching my thigh to snap out of it, I can't hide the grimace that escapes.

"I said I like your name. It suits you." His head cocks to the side, the longer strands falling over his eyes. "Are you okay, little one?"

"I'm fine." Snapping at him, I grind my teeth. "Just because I'm short that doesn't mean I'm little."

"It is a ... how do you say it?" His gaze flicks up in thought before dropping to my face with a glint of satisfaction. His fingers click together before he points a finger at me. "An endearment."

"It's an insult dude, not an endearment." I deadpan and he grins at me. "If I'm not mistaken"—I know for damn sure I'm not but I'll die if he knows how many times I've said his name, asleep or awake—"your name is Ethan, right?"

"Étienne." His blue eyes narrow as if daring me to butcher his name with my American accent again. For some stupid reason, I rise to the challenge.

"Ethen, got it." A muscle twitches in his chiseled jaw and my lips stretch into a wide enough smile to hurt my cheeks. Salmon moves and brings me back to the present, all humor draining from me. "Why are you here?"

"I came to your rescue." Looking around as if seeing the room for the first time, he brings those blue orbs to rest on my face again.

"You can get me out of here?" Too afraid to hope, I hold my breath while waiting for his answer. The line forming between his eyebrows does not look very promising. He still looks hotter than the sun, though, damn him.

"I would think so."

Instead of reassuring me, he looks at Salmon like the cat is in charge here. I should've known he is as bat shit crazy as I am. Hot or not, if anyone waits for a cat to make a decision they have gone off the rails. Way off the rails. I don't want to think about what that says about me. Nope, no thank you.

"He is a cat," I say it slowly like he has difficulty comprehending words.

"I know that." His shoulders stiffen and he jerkily brushes spiderwebs off his shirt and pants that I don't notice until now. "Not an ordinary one, but a cat none the less."

"You can say that twice." Salmon bares his sharp teeth at us but I ignore him. "Listen, I don't mean to be rude or anything but I'm kinda being held here against my will. I'm not sure when Seraphina will be back, so if you are going to

Sound

rescue me—for which I'm very grateful by the way and can't thank you enough—we should scram. Like now, preferably."

"Right." With a sharp nod, he glances around again while I watch him expectantly.

It's adorable how his too-perfect face takes an aura of leadership. I almost snap my heels and salute him. Before I realize what he is planning, he snatches my hand, sending tingles up my arm when our skin connects. His feet falter, his head snapping in my direction, but I'm not sure if he felt it too or if my gasp makes him turn my way. My heart skips a beat when his eyes bore into mine with such intensity I don't think I can breathe. Salmon releases a high-pitched meow, which shatters the moment. I'm not sure if I want to kiss the cat or kick him all the way to Sunday.

"This way." His deep voice raises goosebumps on my arms.

My tongue peeks out to wet my dry lips as he leads me toward the wall. I should feel urgency and excitement knowing I'll be out of here but all that is tamped down by the awareness of how close he is to me.

Just as he reaches the wall, my brain comes back online and I dig my heels in while yanking on his hand.

"No, we can't go now." There is so much panic in my voice he stops suddenly, peering at me over his shoulder.

Or looking down at me over his shoulder I should say.

"My friends." I hurry to explain in case he changes his mind and leaves. "They are here, too. I'm not sure where but I see both of them every time Seraphina makes me play. I can't leave them here, please."

Indecision is plastered all over his face when his gaze roams from me to the closed door behind me and back. He will leave me here. I can feel it in my bones. Unshed tears sting my eyes and blur his face. A lump forms in my throat the size of a tennis ball. His gaze flicks to Salmon, who is sitting patiently at my feet. I duck my head and let the hair fall over to cover my face. No need for him to see me crying. I look pathetic enough as it is.

"Do you know where to find them?"

My head jerks up, hope blooming in my chest. But he is not looking at me. The question is aimed at Salmon and my brain short circuits. The cat brought him here? As if this night hasn't been weird enough. I look at Salmon as well. He glares at us, his tail flicking in agitation.

"I'd say that's a no." When Étienne's eyes meet mine, I press my lips tight. "He does that tail thing when he doesn't like something." As if I make perfect sense, he nods and glances at the door again.

"We can come back for them later." I stare at him for a long time before he sighs. "I don't know what we are dealing with here. I detest magic and witches. If we go searching now, I might not be able to protect you or get you out of here tonight." His eyes soften when I swallow thickly. "We will come back for them, I promise."

God help me but I believe him.

I've had trust issues my whole life but there is no doubt in my mind that he speaks the truth, or that he really means it. The problem is this: do I dare leave Viola and Harmony here until we can manage to get them out of here? What if it takes a while? What if we can't find them?

"What if she hurts them because I escaped?" Voicing my biggest fear, my fingers tighten on his hand like that will stop me from falling apart.

"You would stay to protect your friends?" He searches my face for something but I have no idea what.

With a herculean effort, I uncurl my stiff fingers from

his hand and take a step back. Everything in me screams to grab him and run to wherever he takes me, but the pale, wide-eyed faces of my friends float like ghosts in front of my eyes. I can't do that to them. I can't just leave.

"Yes. I'm sorry." Taking another step I fight the tears that want to spill out. "I'll never be able to live with myself if something happens to them."

A rustle of fabric and a scuff of feet comes from behind the closed door. My stomach drops to my feet and I can see Étienne fighting with himself to stay or go. My heart warms because I know he will stay with me if I ask him, facing whatever the bitch throws his way, but it breaks at the same time because of what I'm about to do. No one will get hurt because of me. Not my friends or him. With a sad smile, I launch forward and shove his chest as hard as I can. Eyes widening, he falls back and disappears through the wall.

The door opens behind me.

Chapter Ten

Étienne

Choking down the growl so I don't make a sound and give myself away, I jump to my feet, somehow ignoring the wet pants sticking to the back of my thighs and ass. I should've known this girl is like no other female I've dealt with before. The first time I saw her she knocked down two human males by hitting them across the head with her violin case. I found it amazing at the time, the fire in her eyes as she stood there daring them to mess with her.

Grimacing, I glance down at myself. I don't find it so amazing at the moment.

Something brushes against my leg and I see the cat as quiet as a whisper threading around my feet while he stares up at me, his orange eyes glowing in the darkness of the tunnel. I guess he doesn't want to be seen by the magic user either, not that I blame the cat. Melody said it was a he. Salmon, she called him. My lips twitch, my smile threatening to appear more times tonight than ever before. The slamming of a door wipes it out completely. Grinding my teeth, I lean as close as I dare, as if that will help in any way.

"Who are you talking to, girl?" a familiar voice I cannot place snarls on the other side.

"Myself." Melody's soft words tighten my chest. "I'm always alone, so if I don't talk to someone I'll forget how to speak, sorry."

"There is no need for you to speak. All you have to do is play that instrument. Haven't you learned that by now?" The voice sounds louder, so I assume whoever the female speaking is she has moved closer to the wall I'm hiding behind. *Like a coward.* The snide remark in my mind stabs my pride.

"Yes ma'am." The docile way Melody speaks contradicts everything I know about the girl, which is not much I guess. Still, it rubs me wrong to hear it.

"Drink," the female snaps, the word like acid dripping from her mouth. "That's it, all the way to the bottom. I said all of it."

Fists clenching, I swallow the mouthful of blood where my fangs pierce the inside of my mouth. My entire body is stiff, muscles bunched and ready to rip the magic user to shreds. The only thing holding me back is the uncertainty of whether Melody will be safe or get hurt in the process. I may have just met the girl, but the idea of hurting her makes me want to roar and destroy the world.

"If it wasn't for what you are and that stupid violin, you'd be useless." The female sneers just as something bangs on a wall further away. "There you go, sleep. You'll give me more of your life tomorrow." Chuckling like a deranged clown, she moves away, her voice fading with her. "Disgusting creatures, the lot of you. And they thought they could hide you among humans to make sure not even you know what you are. Not from me they won't. I will take everything you have to give, all of it, until there is nothing left from you."

I stand frozen, my mind reeling while the female laughs, the excitement clear in her tone before I hear the thud of the door closing. The lock clicks next, leaving only silence behind. I don't dare move, let alone breathe. The cat brushes against my leg again and I recoil from it. The words from the magic user ring in my head on repeat. *"They thought they could hide you among humans to make sure not even you know what you are."* That means the girl doesn't know she's not human.

It means she doesn't know I'm not human.

Will she fear me if she knows what I am? For some reason that is more important than anything else to me right now. When the silence stretches for long enough, I force all thoughts away and step back into the room. My heart kicks my breastbone when I don't see Melody standing where I expect to see her. My gaze darts around the room before finding her half-draped on the tiny bed, one leg and arm hanging limply to the side. Rushing to her, I turn her on her back, smoothing the hair away from her face. Her lashes flutter and open slightly, a small smile playing on her lips.

The fangs throb in my mouth.

"You came back," she whispers, those full lips tilted at the corners begging to be kissed. She looks sleepy, as if she has just woken up. "I'm glad."

"I'll always come back for you." The words are out before I can stop them and I'm shocked to find I really mean them.

Sound

I have never made a promise like that to anyone but my brothers. Not even to my father. So what does that say about this girl? She might be more dangerous to me than the magic user and the assassins put together. With her doll-like looks and sweet innocence, she will make me her willing victim. My fist tightens in her hair.

A perfect weapon.

What I have before me is the perfect weapon to end my bloodline. Will she have the same effect on Lucien and Moël? Unable to stop it, the possessive growl vibrates from my chest. Melody giggles and lifts her hand, her fingers tracing my lips.

"Those stupid drugs make me hallucinate, Ethan." My cock presses hard against the zipper of my pants when her fingers rub my fangs. Unaware, I peel my lips back and snarl in her face, eliciting a giggle from her. "They makes me think you are a vampire." Snorting ungracefully, she keeps rubbing my mouth.

Snatching her hands, I press them on the side of her head, which puts us face to face. Her pupils dilate, her breathing speeding up as she licks her lips. Panting like an animal above her, I'm disgusted at myself that all I want to do right now is rip her clothes off and bury my fangs in her neck while shoving my cock inside her. It's obvious she has been drugged and is not herself. My mind knows that, but my body ... not so much. Pushing the instincts away, I try to release her but her fingers lace through mine and hold me back. A lesser male will stay and do what she asks of him. It's a moment of truth for me.

I am a lesser male.

"Kiss me." Her half-lidded gaze is locked on my mouth, fascination swirling in it.

"You are not yourself, Melody." I don't move away, my

eyes flicking to her glistening lips. "You will hate me for it later."

"Kiss me anyway." The breathy sound of her voice almost makes me spill in my pants.

Cursing under my breath, I look away from her face. She is turning my resolve to do right by her into dust. My eyes land on three red welts on the creamy skin of her forearm. By the looks of it, Salmon left his mark on her. I will definitely skin that cat ... later. With the urge to taste her too strong to resist, I lower my head and brush my lips over the three scratches. The scent of blooming roses and the coppery zing of her blood burn my nostrils. With a low growl at the back of my throat, I flatten my tongue and lick her skin.

A soft moan passes her lips, the skin under my nose pebbling up. Her back arches, pushing her breasts to my chest. So I don't do anything stupid like bite her and drink her until she is part of me, I bury my face in the crook of her neck. The scratches on her skin burn the back of my eyelids and push at my instincts to mark her as well, to erase the claim the damn cat has made.

"You won't kiss me, will you?" Melody sighs, relaxing under me.

"Ask me again tomorrow," I tell her hair, my lips grazing the skin of her shoulder.

"You are no fun, pretty boy." She sounds so petulant I almost laugh. "Not that I blame you. You can have any woman you want, so why would you kiss me."

Taken aback by her comment, I lift my head to find she actually believes her words. Throwing caution and my morals to the wind, I fist her hair and yank her face to mine. I swallow her startled gasp and the low moan she releases,

Sound

pushing my tongue past her lips. I devour her mouth like a starving male. Her flavor explodes on my taste buds making me drunk from it, from her. Her tiny fingers claw at my shoulders to bring me closer to her and I barely manage to stop the insanity overtaking my rational mind. Pulling back, I give her one soft peck on her lower lip before lifting my head to look at her.

"Holy shit." She breathes, looking dazed. Not that I feel much better myself.

"Ask me again to kiss you tomorrow," I tell her, unable to look away from her swollen lips.

"You can bet your pretty ass I'm going to ask. That was … it was … " her words trail off.

"A small kiss." With a wink, I grin at her.

"Wow, smug much?" Snickering, her gaze keeps flicking to my lips. "I think I'm going to die tomorrow from embarrassment when the drugs wear off."

"Don't worry, I'll remind you." My grin grows when she squints at me, her eyes turning to slits.

"I think I liked you better when you didn't speak English."

"I always spoke English, you just assumed I didn't." Her rosy cheeks warm my heart for some stupid reason. "I will let you sleep it off, little one. I'll go look for a way to find your friends so we can get you out of here."

"Promise?" she murmurs sleepily, her eyes fluttering closed.

"I promise." She sighs at my words and falls asleep.

With great reluctance, I lift off her, tucking her in under the threadbare blanket. I don't want to walk away and leave her behind, but the sooner I figure out how to find her friends the sooner I can take her home with me. I stumble away from her at the thought of her in my home. Her peaceful face tightens my chest. Yes, no way I'm letting her slip through my fingers. The girl is mine whether she knows it yet or not.

"Fuck me." Huffing a breath out, I rub my face.

I better find that damn cat.

Chapter Eleven

Melody

Waking up to find Étienne gone was a relief. I had the strangest dream to date where his beautiful face was looming over mine and fangs as long as my pinky were poking out of his lips. His too-blue eyes glowed from within like lanterns and his cheekbones had a sharper edge to them, giving him an even more perfect look. And he was kissing me like he was trying to fuse his mouth to mine and stay like that forever. He kissed me because I asked him to. No, scratch that, I begged him to do it. My face feels hot enough to fry an egg on it at the thought.

My fingers reach up, rubbing my still-swollen lips and telling me it wasn't really a dream. Well, not all of it at least. I'm sure he didn't sprout fangs out of nowhere or flip a switch to make his eyes glow. The drugs mess with my head; I know that. No matter what, though, I can't wipe the stupid smile off my face.

"He kissed me," I tell Salmon, who is glaring at me from across the room.

Not even the bad-tempered cat can sour my mood. Right now, I don't think even Seraphina can kill the buzzing in my chest. Flopping back on the bed, I sigh. I might not have much experience, but that kiss was out of this world. I think he messed me up for any other guy. The expectations went sky high with this girl. I'm no virgin—although the memory of my non-virginhood is better left forgotten—but I've never felt like that in my life. Like he was trying to leave a stamp on my soul to say he has been there. Another sigh follows as I stare at the cracks on the ceiling, my arm limply hanging off the bed. A wet nose bumps at it and I roll over to peek at Salmon.

"You are not upset with me anymore?" My fingers wiggle under his chin and the purring starts. "I should say thank you, Salmon. He said you brought him here."

The cat grumbles and I pick him up, setting him on my stomach, which tightens as he kneads the shirt before nesting against me and curling in a ball. One hand gliding over his silky fur, I just breathe. It feels like a long time has passed since my chest hasn't been weighed down with fear or worry. I don't know if it's because he promises he will be back, or from the kiss. Maybe a mixture of both? I don't know and I don't care. Either way, I'll take it.

The door flings open so suddenly it slams the opposite wall bouncing off it. I bolt upright, dropping Salmon on the floor. Thankfully he lands on four paws, but I'm not sure where I'm about to land. Seraphina, her face twisted in rage, stands at the threshold, hands fisted at her sides. I recoil from the hatred burning in her amber gaze.

Salmon, arching his back and tail sticking up like an antenna on his butt hisses at her.

Sound

"I knew you were not talking to yourself."

Spitting the words like venom, she marches inside. Before I can move, she kicks Salmon so hard the poor cat flies out the door with a shrieking meow. The loud thump against the wall in the hallway is like a hot poker to my chest. Ignoring the consequences, I bolt out the door and scoop the cat into my arms. The poor thing is shivering, clinging to my chest while his claws scratch my skin. My whole body is vibrating with tremors as well.

"Release him." A hand grabs a fistful of my hair, yanking my head back. "I said release him!" She is pulling so hard she'll snap my neck. My arms fall limply to my sides on their own.

Fear chokes me. I have no control over my body and the cat is clinging to my shirt, his claws ripping the fabric as his weight pulls him down. With another loud shrieking meow, Salmon pushes off my body and drops a couple of feet away, bolting down the hallway. I'm yanked back inside the room.

Chunks of hair are pulled out of my skull while Seraphina guides me to the bed. Shoving me on it hard, I hit my hip on the metal frame so hard I see stars. Tears burn my eyes but I push them away. I will not cry in front of her.

"So, Alto thought it was smart to disobey me," she says conversationally.

"Who?" Pushing the hair off my face, I look at her.

"He was not allowed near any of you. I see he needs a lesson in obedience."

"The cat?" Afraid she will hurt the poor thing, I drop at her feet, pleading with her. "It's not his fault. I tricked him to come here because I was bored. Please don't hurt him."

"My oh my, what have we here?" She glares down her nose at me. "A cat you say?"

"Yes, it was my fault. He didn't want to come at first." Not understanding her glee, I stay kneeling in hopes she will change her mind.

Seraphina strides to the door, stopping with one foot on either side of the threshold. "Alto! Get your furry ass in here now." Her shout makes me cringe.

I guess that's the cat's real name and I hope he is hiding somewhere. No animal will come back after a kick like the one she gave him. To my shock, the cat appears, edging past Seraphina warily. She grins at it like a fiend, her foot twitching in a mocking kick. The cat bolts inside the room and stops near me, but this time he doesn't hide.

"Melody here"—Her upper lip curls like my name tastes bad in her mouth—"thinks you are a cat. Shall we enlighten her?"

Salmon—or Alto as she calls him—shrinks back pinning his ears to the back of his head. I'm confused as all hell, so I gap at both of them. Sitting back on my haunches, I look from the cat to Seraphina. The bitch is enjoying this too much so I know whatever is coming next will not bode well for me ... or the cat.

"You see, Alto here was just like you once. Weren't you, Alto?" When no one answers, she continues. "After he served his purpose, I had no other use for him apart from turning him into my familiar. This way I can use him until the day he dies, which will be a long, long time from now if I have anything to say about it."

"What?" Yeah, I know. Not a very eloquent question, but my mind is blank after what I heard.

"Let me show you." Seraphina looks absolutely delighted, while I'm trying hard not to scream.

Sound

"Indica mihi quid occulti oculos." Her arms lift in front of her, a reddish glow spreading like snakes from her fingers. Her words are as understandable to me as if she spoke English, the old kind you'd find in faded poetry tomes. *"Show me what thou hast hidden from the eyes of the."*

That same reddish glow surrounds the cat and the form shimmers like looking at it through water. It pulses and twists until it curls up, swirling before revealing a handsome guy around my age. His brown eyes are wide, horror written all over his face. Longish blond hair tied in a low ponytail rests over one shoulder, contrasting with the black jacket he wears. His lips part as if to speak, but the glow covers him like a cloud again, changing him back to a cat only a moment later.

"Oh my God," I breathe the words, tears falling unchecked down my face.

"Your God has nothing to do with it." Seraphina sneers down at me where I'm still kneeling. "I am your god now. Take a good look at the *cat*, as you like to call him. That will also be your fate."

She whirls out of the room after dropping that bomb, leaving me staring at Alto. I'm not a hundred percent sure if it's for him or me, but he looks miserable. Brushing off the tears with jerky swipes of my hands, I offer him a sad smile. I will not look at him with pity because he deserves more than that.

"Alto, get your ass out of the room right now," she snaps from the hallway, and I watch him padding gently after her, his head and tail hanging limply down.

I stare at the locked door for a long time after they are gone.

Chapter Twelve

Étienne

"You look like something chewed you up and spit you out."

I've ignored the squishy sounds my shoes are making all the way home, but I doubt that will work on Lucien. I'm still willing to try. When he doesn't get an answer to his comment, he falls in step with me, sniffing gingerly in my direction.

"You smell like shit."

"Thank you."

Passing the open foyer, I take the stairs two at a time. Leaving dirt and grime wherever I step, I can't help but think that Moël will have a blast. My younger brother—the ruthless assassin of my court—finds cleaning soothing. Who would've thought? As long as I don't have to do it, he can have at it. Swinging the door to my bedroom open, I reach back and pull the shirt over my head. When I turn around to close the door, I come face to face with Lucien. He doesn't get the hint to leave me alone.

Sound

"Care to share where you were?" Bracing on the doorframe, he looks at me expectantly.

"What are you, my mother now?" I crow, but he doesn't budge. "I need a shower. We can talk when I'm done."

Lucien nods. Sighing, I take a step back so I can close the door. Shouldering past me, he saunters in my space and drapes over a chair. Entwining fingers over his stomach, he stares evenly at me.

"You can wait for me in the office." The metal groans where I'm squeezing the crap out of the door knob.

"I'm good." The heel of his shitkickers hits the low table in front of him, his other leg following until they cross at the ankles. "I'll be right here when you're ready to start talking."

"I will be right down ..."

"Go get on with it." Shooing me with his hand, he squirms in the chair as if getting more comfortable. "I'll hear you just fine from here."

Grinding my teeth, I ball up the shirt and chuck it in the open hamper in the corner of the room. Unbuckling, I kick off my shoes before dropping my pants and stepping out of them. Lucien lifts an eyebrow at my nudity, which tells me if I think that will get to him I'm sorely mistaken. Cursing him in my head, I stride to the bathroom and yank none too gently on the screen door. The spray of water blasts out next, so I step in and slam the door closed.

Bracing my arms on the tiles, I let my head hang low on my chest and the hot water pound into my neck and shoulders. I still feel unsettled from everything tonight, but mostly from that kiss. I can't get the feel and taste of her out of my mind. Swinging my arm back, I punch the wall with a furious roar. My fist goes through tile and brick, shredding the skin on my knuckles.

I welcome the pain.

"I found the loophole." I hate that Lucien knows I'll sing like a canary, yet I can't stop myself from talking. "That damn cat is not trying to trick us."

I'm not certain if that's true but I'm fifty percent convinced it's not luring us into a trap. Fifty is better than what I have at the beginning of this, so I'll go with it. I'm just not sure if I'm trying to convince myself or my brother. Lucien stays quiet, so I continue to fill the silence like a sinner confessing his sins.

"I walked through the wards and entered the place."

"You did what now?" My brother is looming at the open door of the bathroom, anger rolling off him in waves.

"I needed to know," I tell him simply. "I knew if I was trapped in there the two of you would get me out."

"You bet your ass we would but only so I could kick some sense into your thick head. What the hell is the matter with you, Étienne?" Spitting the words, he steps inside. "You could've died by the time we found you. You are a goddamn heir to the throne!" The roared words bounce of the tiles and echo in the bathroom.

"You are only pissed because that responsibility will fall on you if I kick the bucket."

His pissed-off growl makes me smile. Remembering why we are having this awkward conversation with me naked in the shower, I tiredly push the water off my face.

"The girl is trapped there, Lucien." My heart kicks hard against my breastbone. "She needs help."

"A lot of humans get trapped as a result of their own stupidity. That's never been our problem. They can deal with their own." Spitting the words, he walks out and I hear the chair groaning when he plops down.

Sound

Taking a deep breath, I blow it out slowly. Here goes nothing.

"She is not human."

"Say what now?" He's back, this time so close to the glass door I can clearly see the scowl on his face.

"She is not human." I grab the soap, needing to wash this night off my skin, and so I don't have to face him. "And she is mine."

"Hang on there ... whoa ... hold on just a minute... putain de bordel de merde! " Stuttering before reverting to French, he hisses out every vile word he has ever learned.

I wait him out, scrubbing at my skin until its raw.

"Is she one of us?" After he has exhausted his explicit vocabulary, he holds his breath while waiting for my answer.

"No." Before he starts again, I hurry to say my peace. "I don't know what she is but the witch has her trapped and is using her somehow. I'm sure it has something to do with the music."

"The music ..." Lucien murmurs distractedly. "We need Moël here too. This has gone way over our heads."

"I heard everything." My youngest brother speaks from somewhere in my bedroom. "So what's the plan?"

"You are not going along with his stupidity, are you?" Lucien rounds Moël, walking out of the bathroom. "He doesn't even know what she is and he thinks he found his mate."

"Who are we to tell fate how to pair up souls, Lucien?" My shoulders relax at Moël's carefree tone. "Mate or not, you think we should look away from a female in danger? It's not like there are lot of them floating around."

They continue talking but I tune them out. What Moël says is true. Every century, there are less and less females in all species, minus humans of course. After washing my hair,

I turn off the water and step out. A cloud of steam follows behind me when I snatch a towel off the rack and sling it over my hips.

"She could be one of the Fae," Moël mumbles. "They are all about music and what have you."

"She is a tiny little thing," I tell him as I head for the closet. "You could be right on that count."

"I've never heard of a Fae being mated to one of us." Lucien keeps poking where he shouldn't. "Last time I checked, they hated us."

Stabbing my feet into a new pair of pants, I yank them up. Everything in me wants to roar so the world knows she is mine. I don't understand it myself, but I don't question it. Fae or human, I do not care. I'm getting her out of there. Pulling a shirt over my head, I walk out and stop in front of Lucien.

"I didn't ask for your help, nor do I have a wish to involve you in this." He eyes me strangely, his body stopping all movement. A predator facing another predator. "I told you she is mine. That makes her my problem and no one else's."

"I don't know about Lucien, but I'm in." When Lucien glares at Moël, my younger brother shrugs a shoulder. "That place is strange. I'd like to see why. Helping Étienne is just a bonus. I was going to go there anyway."

"Have it your way." All the fight leaves Lucien and he rubs the top of his head. "But I have a bad feeling about this. At least if we go down we will do it together. Just like old times."

"Just like old times." Moël grins, probably remembering our younger days when the court had no peace from the troubles we caused. That is what I'm remembering now, too.

Sound

"Now what?" Lucien looks from me to Moël.

"I'm going back there." I haven't been back for an hour and I'm already itching to see her again. "You can search through the texts we have, see if you can find anything that might explain what she is."

"On it." Jumping off the chair, Lucien is gone before I register his eagerness to help, which isn't easy anyways since only two minutes ago he was going for my neck.

"He worries about you, he just doesn't know how to show it." Moël chuckles. "You know those large dogs? The ones that could break your bones, but you still want to sit on your lap and cuddle? That's Lucien in a nutshell."

"I'm afraid to ask how you know about large dogs wanting to cuddle."

"TV, brother. Humans did one thing right and that's Netflix. You should try it." Snickering, he heads for the door.

"I'm good, thank you." Watching him go, I swallow my pride. "Moël?"

"Hmm?" Glancing over his shoulder, his scar pulls on the skin of his face. A lump forms in my throat.

"If I'm not back in a day, don't come there."

"If you are not back in half a day, I will level that place to the ground." With a nod, he walks out of the room. "Go get your female, brother."

Chapter Thirteen

Melody

My legs are getting numb where I'm still kneeling on the floor, the cold seeping into my bones. The knot that is loosened in my chest returns with a vengeance, like a physical pain spreading through my ribs. It's one thing to know that magic is real and to see glimpses of it, like the golden rope snaking out from my chest to Seraphina's. Somehow, I convince myself that what I'm seeing is a trick of the light, or just my frightened brain making things up because I'm scared out of my mind. It's a totally different story when a cat is transformed into a human being right in front of my eyes.

I feel numb.

When the pain in my chest becomes unbearable, I suck in a lungful of air, the shock of it all blocking even the basic motor skills my body has … like breathing. Sharp pain spears through me, and I can feel it all the way to my back. Blinking fast, my head moves slowly to look around the room as if I'm seeing it for the first time. What am I doing? My shaking fingers thread through the hair falling around my face and tuck it behind my ear. I realize all this time I block everything I can't explain, purposely ignoring it like it doesn't exist. It is easier to deal with the situation this way. Otherwise, I may think I'm insane.

I'm not crazy, am I?

Everything is very much real, even if my rational mind can't explain it. Fear of the pain she inflicts keeps me between these walls allowing her to do whatever she wants to do. Until I end up like Alto. Because apparently being turned into an animal is what comes next in this fantastical world I find myself in. Pinching my thigh so hard my eyes water from the pain does not wake me from this nightmare I'm stuck in.

No, this is real.

Magic is real.

My eyes lock on the violin propped on the chair. I remember dropping it when I had been forced to play it, yet here it sits. Back where it always waits for me, day and night. I can barely feel my heart, not sure if it's even beating as I crawl on my hands and knees on the floor, moving closer to it. The moment my fingers touch it, warmth spreads through my hand, up my arm, and through the rest of my body. It's like the instrument is alive and giving me a hug. I've always felt the sensation, but right now it takes a whole different meaning. This is not just my excitement of playing or my love for music. This is something else.

Snatching my hand back, I eye the violin like it may come alive and bite me. Stranger things happen every day, to be sure. Blowing out a long breath until my chest caves in on itself, I turn around to look at the room again. At my prison. What am I doing here? The question pops up again as my gaze travels over stained walls and simple furniture. I keep telling myself I'm biding my time until I can find a way to escape, but that is just the lie I create so I don't give up. Either way, I know the truth. There is no escape for me.

There is no running from magic, from Seraphina.

My pathetic heart jumps once and kicks my ribs hard when my eyes stop on the part of the wall where Étienne disappeared. Do I dare follow through it? Can I live with myself if I leave Viola and Harmony behind knowing the same fate waits for them too? Another thought comes with that. If both of them are in the same situation as me, that means I'm not responsible for all those people dying. My two friends have the same curse as I do. Our music is cursed, and that should make me feel a little better.

It doesn't.

Limbs trembling, tremors raking over my spine and clawing at my insides, I lift off the floor. Some primal part of my brain kicks in, and with one fast glance at the violin I turn my back to it. It won't help anyone—definitely not Viola or Harmony—if I'm stuck here myself. I should've listened to Étienne and left with him when I had a chance, especially since he promised to come back for them anyways. It's not too late, right? I'll go through that wall and hide somewhere until he comes back. At least I won't be here. And he did say he will come back.

Urgency rushes over me, coursing through my veins. The thought of being out of this place is so overwhelming I'm afraid to move. If I do, it may shatter the fragile hold I have over the sliver of hope still alive inside of me. My chest is rising and falling fast, my gaze darting left and right as panic chokes me like a fist squeezing my throat.

"You can do this, Melody." Voice cracking from emotion, the words whisper through my numb lips. Determination burns hot and bright with each breath I take. "I can do this."

The shock wears off, releasing me from the frozen state I'm in. Remembering Étienne and the shape of his clothing when he was here, I look down at my bare feet. My eyes snap at the boots, the only footwear I have here. One is still next to the chair where it always is, and after swiveling my head around, I find the other across from me closer to the foot of my bed. Snatching the one closest to me, I rush to grab the other. The high heels are good to use as a weapon, but they'll be horrible if I'm trying to sneak out of here.

The blood is rushing through me, buzzing in my ears like I'm in the middle of a tornado. My feet slap on the floor with the couple of steps it takes me to get to the desk with all the makeup on it. Gripping the toes of one boot, I lift it over my head, smashing the heel down on the wood as hard as I can. Bottles of foundation, lipstick, and mascara jump from it and sail through the air. The loud thump locks my muscles in a vise.

I freeze.

The air is cold where I snort it fast through my nose, hyperventilating from fear that Seraphina has heard the noise. Straining my ears is useless because I can't hear a damn thing from the fast beating of my heart that lodged itself in my throat like a lump. Eyes wide enough to pop out of my head, I stare at the door expecting her to storm in and kill me. Deep down I know if she catches me she won't think twice about it. Now that I know Viola and Harmony must be the same as me, she doesn't really need me, does she? She has two more that she can force to play. Two others she can turn into cats.

Hysterical giggles spew from my mouth, the sound foreign and crazed.

When nothing happens and no murderous bitch storms through the door with magic aimed at my head, I tighten my hold on my boots. The bed pokes at my brain from the corner of my eye, so I turn my gaze to it. The metal frame stares at me accusingly as if calling me all sorts of stupid. Clenching my teeth, hearing them grind loud enough to raise the hair on my arms, I walk up to it and press one knee on the thin, hard mattress. Lifting the boot as high as I can over my head, I bring it down on the metal as hard as I can, putting all my body weight behind it. The thin heel snaps off and flies away. It hits the wall then bounces off it, making me duck as the damn thing almost stabs my eye. Not waiting, I switch to the other boot and do the same to it. This heel goes flying too, but it lands at the foot of the bed when it ricochets off the wall.

My tail bone sends a stabbing pain up my spine when I sit too close to the edge of the bed. Ignoring it, I shove my feet in the boots and zip them up, my eyes not moving from the closed door. Adrenaline raises goosebumps all over my body.

So close. I'm so close to freedom.

Jumping up, I grab the one broken-off heel in my hand and, without waiting, bolt straight at the door. There is a moment where my brain screams at me to stop, tells me I'll slam my face in the wall the closer it comes to my face, but I squeeze my eyes shut and hold my breath, not allowing myself to stop. A ripple passes over my body, my skin tightening like a sunburn under it. One second my muscles stiffen expecting impact with the wall, and the next misty air washes over me. It smells horrible but I've never inhaled better tasting air in my life. My eyes snap open and darkness greets me, shooting panic through my head. I stand frozen for just a second, my feet squashing under me before the reason I'm in this darkness kicks in. A wide grin stretches my lips so much my face hurts. Sucking in a shuddering breath, clutching the broken heel in my hand so hard the chipped edge bites my skin, I blot through the darkness. Two steps are all I take. Crippling pain makes the eyes roll to the back of my head and I drop on the ground, my cheek sinking into a mushy goo. My brain screams no but I can't take a breath.

The darkness swallows me.

Chapter Fourteen

Étienne

Crouched on the roof of a building, I'm debating the wisdom of coming on foot. I have every intention of bringing Melody home with me. The more I think about it, the more the roots of that thought sink deeper into my brain. I walked out of that cursed place once without her, leaving her at the mercy of the witch without a clue what I may find when I return. I'm not sure I can do it a second time.

Jumping the few stories down, my knees bend slightly to soften the impact before I'm out and away from the stench of the alley. It's a good thing this part of town has been deserted, leaving just a handful of residents still clinging to it. Those that remain either have no other place to go or are hiding secrets of their own from the rest of the humans.

It's almost dawn, the sky lightening with each step I take. It'll be monumentally stupid if I get stuck outside

Sound

hiding from irrelevant humans so the sun can kill me before I reach her.

Gathering the mist around me like a cloak, my boots beat an even rhythm on the streets. My heart thumps in sync with it as I weave through buildings and broken-apart homes until my eyes land on the ancient church, its depleted walls and broken windows the best sight I've seen in a long time. My feet move faster as I streak across the street and round the ruined place.

Stumbling when a sharp pain zings through my chest, I catch myself just before my hand slaps the wall next to me. With hands pressed on my thighs, I clench my jaw and breathe through my nose until the pain subsides. I have no idea what that agony is but I do know the pain is not my own. It isn't from my brothers, either. That only leaves one other.

"Melody." Jolting upright, I push all the pain away.

Sharp blades tear my gut as I rush to the place I used for an entrance, fear for her life choking the air in my lungs. She can't be hurt. I will lose my shit if a hair is missing from her head. All rational thought leaves my mind as my instincts take over. The lightening sky turns shades of reds and greens, which scares the shit out of me. I've never reacted to anything this way, my body moving of its own accord as if a part of myself I don't know exists is taking over.

The predator in me rejoices at the burning pain of the wards as I pass through and enter the dark tunnel. The colors swirl, dancing in front of my eyes as I move through it, not bothered a second by the nasty scent or sludge covering everything. I can always see through the dark, my genetic makeup assuring I can see my prey. This is different.

Darkness comes alive around me, the colors of my

vision lighting the intricate weaving of the wards as well. Slowing down, I let my eyes roam where the links have been broken to forge this passage. The cobweb of magic has been pinned to the sides with a golden thread five strings thick. Silver puffs of magic pop in and out through the golden strings like musical notes showing themselves before disappearing again. They playfully twinkle around me, guiding me along the path the same way the cat did when he led me here.

Is this the cat's doing?

Shaking my head to disperse the enchantment the notes are weaving through my head, I look straight ahead keeping my gaze pinned to the ground. If I keep staring at them, I'll be stuck here forever. Melody needs me now. I've wasted enough time.

Forcing my feet to move, I walk deeper inside the tunnel. It's much different from the first time I was here in a lot of ways, and it's not just my vision. The air gets thicker the deeper I go like it's doing its best to stop me from getting closer. Shoulders hunching, I lock my muscles and push through, moving as sluggishly as a drunk human. Everything in me wants to let go of any rational thought and tear this place apart. For her sake, I hold onto my sanity with all I've got.

Do it! a primal part of my brain urges with a chuckle. *Let her see you for what you are so her human brain can tell her to run. Show her the monster that you are so that she can fear you.*

My nails dig in the skin where I'm clenching my fists, my forearms bunching like stone under my shirt. A muscle is ticking on the side of my jaw as I push forward dragging one foot in front of the other. Other thoughts come too, tormenting me with everything that has eaten me alive through the years after my father's death. All the ways I wasn't fit to take his place.

I couldn't save him.

You can't save her either.

A feral growl vibrates my chest as I push that treacherous thought away. I will save her if it's the last thing I do. It might ease the guilt I've carried for so long, at least some of it. It might give meaning to my useless existence, at least for a little while. The fact that I can barely move right now —little less get Melody out of here—is something I refuse to acknowledge. I'll figure it out when I get to her.

Rounding the elbow of the tunnel where it curves to the right, every thought disappears from my mind. There in front of me, close to the end, a lump is raising from the ground. No, not a lump. One pale hand is flung to the side, the fingers disappearing in the sludge covering the floor. Fear like a living thing surges through me, dispersing everything but my need to get to Melody. Her lifeless body is sprawled in the gunk like a broken doll.

One moment I'm far enough away that I can barely make out her form, and the next my knees hit the ground where her head is pressed down, her hair covering her face. Yanking her up, I push at the dark strands, my trembling hand smoothing them away as I drink her in. Mud covers her right cheek, sliding down to her neck. Leaning closer, I lower my ear to her lips and press my palm to the center of her chest. There is no breath passing through her lungs and no heartbeat meets my hand.

Panic short-circuits my brain, freezing me in place. It's not just her lifeless body I'm holding in my hands. It's my father's too. Her face and his flickers in front of my unseeing eyes, changing from one to the other and tainting my incompetence to do anything for either of them.

Unaware of what I'm doing, desperation claws at me as I jump to my feet and cradle her to my chest. Her body hangs loose in my arms, her limbs and head flipping around with my jerky movements. Turning my back to put her room behind us, I bolt down the tunnel the same way I came.

Melody convulses in my arms.

My feet plant on the ground and root me in place. I almost drop her, her body jerking so violently it pushes me to take a few steps back. The convulsions slow down but don't stop. Frowning, I take a couple more steps back. The second I reach the place where I found her she goes limp again.

Not dead.

My knees buckle and I stumble from the relief that thought brings with it. Not wasting more time, I face the moss-ridden wall of the tunnel and step through it into her room. As soon as we pass the barrier, Melody bolts upright in my arms and sucks in a deep breath. I clutch her to my chest, falling on my knees while she gasps, coughs, and claws at my shoulders, but I'm not sure whether she's trying to hold onto me or push me away.

I don't care.

Laughter bursts out from my chest and I squeeze her tight. The galloping of her heart thunders against me, making me feel as weak as a human. *Not dead. She is not dead. I'm not too late.* I keep repeating the thought in my head as I bury my face in her hair. The scent of blooming roses fills my lungs and my whole body moves from the tremors of relief.

"Étienne?" Melody rasps next to my ear.

Chapter Fifteen

Melody

Silence.

I am drowning, my lungs shriveling in my chest where no air is filling them up, and then silence surrounds me. There is nothing there. It is so absolute that not even the panic I know I should be feeling can penetrate it. Alone, I can't even see anything in the all-consuming darkness.

One second, I am nothing, and the next a jolt of energy sends me into a flailing mess, coughing and spitting while sucking in lungful of air. Someone is crushing me to them, their arms of steel wrapping around me like shackles. Thinking it's Seraphina, I kick and claw at her to release me until a familiar voice laughs and a warm face presses to my neck. Blinking fast, my vision clears enough to see a blond head nuzzling where my shoulder meets my neck.

"Étienne?" I wince, my throat feeling raw like I've been chewing on broken glass.

"Melody." The way he says my name, placing the

accent at the end, sends a pleasant shiver through me. The relief in his deep voice soothes my still freaked-out mind. "You are alive, little one."

Lifting his head up, our faces are so close I can feel his breath on my lips. A jolt of something I don't understand slices through me. He looks different. His hair is mussed and wild around his head, the top falling over his forehead. His cheekbones are sharp enough to cut, making him look like he is chiseled out of marble, not skin and bones. His lips are redder than I remember, standing out starkly and forcing me to blink repeatedly, like that will change what I'm seeing. My gaze flicks up, locking on his eyes.

The blue color of the summer skies and calm ocean is gone. Thick, dark lashes lower and lift over pools of molten silver that shimmer and swirl, making me think it's alive. It's Étienne's face in front of me, but something else is watching me through his gaze. Something that is trying to reach in and see to my soul. I should be afraid. Knowing that magic is real, cats can turn into human beings, and being locked here with no way out is enough to drive anyone insane. Thanks to that nightmare, seeing that he is not exactly what I think he is does not come as a shock.

Maybe it should.

Some part of me I don't know is there comes to life. I can feel the thrill and excitement streaming through every nerve ending, purring and stretching with the knowledge that it's being seen. It reacts to whatever lurks behind Étienne's eyes, answering the call while coming to the surface. Like a whole new person, it fills my body and settles under my skin as if it owns it. Everywhere his skin touches mine and every contact between our bodies through the fabric becomes more sensitive. With his body curling around me like a blanket, mine becomes fully aware of his. It's a feeling I can't shake, even if I wanted to.

"Qu'es-tu?" Warm air puffs over my lips when he speaks.

"English," I mumble, unable to look away from him.

"What are you, Melody?" His deep voice vibrates from his chest to mine, his cheek twitching into a flick of a smile. "You are not human."

I startle at his words, a shot of fear piercing me through the chest. I want to rage and scream at him that it's crazy, but after everything that I've been through his words are the only explanation. No matter how ridiculous they may sound. I sure am something, unfortunately human is not the option for me anymore.

Searching the silver moving through his gaze, I swallow thickly. "Neither are you." A line forms between his eyebrows, the thick lashes lowering slightly over his eyes. "Have you seen yourself in the mirror?"

I know I should push him away and get as far away as possible. Melody from a few hours ago would've done that and screamed bloody murder. That part of me seems like it's someone else, someone who was a dream and who finally woke up. I wish I can turn back time and go back to sleep, to have things like they used to be. Étienne's gaze drops to my lips and my mouth goes dry, my stomach flipflopping wildly. Or maybe not. No dream I've ever had can conjure a perfection like the one staring at me as if he is debating if he should kiss me or not.

"You are not human." The tongue sticks to the roof of my mouth but I manage to speak.

"I know I'm not," he tells me dryly, and I can't help but snort at the twist of his mouth. "You are not afraid."

"Should I be?" I challenge him, still not understanding myself why I don't fear him.

"From me?" His eyebrows crawl all the way up to his hairline. "Never."

"I can't leave this place," I blurt out so I don't kiss him.

The longer he holds me in his arms like he will never let me go, the harder it is to resist the urge to seal my lips to his, so I push on his shoulders telling him to let me go without words. He frowns at my weak attempt, but after a few shoves he clenches his jaw and releases me. I can tell it takes great effort on his part and warmth spreads through me. Seeing all his delicious muscles straining the shirt and pants within an inch of their lives brings all my girly bits to life.

"Is that why you were in the tunnel?" Expanding his chest with a deep breath, his jaw works as he struggles to speak. "You were trying to escape?"

"Yes." A lump forms in my throat. "I only managed a couple of steps before pain made me black out."

"You wouldn't leave while I was here but tried to run on your own." The accusation is loud and clear in his deep voice. "Your friends being here had nothing to do with it. You are scared of me."

Curling my legs up and hugging them to my chest, I blow out a breath. Snatching a t-shirt from the bed next to him, he balls it up and wipes the disgusting mud from my face. I let him. As soon as I open my mouth, he will realize I'm crazy and run from here as fast as his legs will carry him. I should lie, tell him I just want to get out of this place, but the hurt I see on his face when he says I'm scared of him makes me sing like a bird.

"I was going to run outside, hide and wait for you until you came back." He narrows those silver eyes, obviously not

Sound

believing my words. "Seraphina found Salmon ..." my voice trails off at the name.

"Seraphina?" Done with cleaning my face, he flicks the shirt aside.

"Seraphina found Alto in the room with me." Ignoring his obvious question of who Seraphina is, I plow through my explanation. "Needless to say, she was not happy about it, so she started kicking him. I begged her to stop, not to hurt him. Then she laughed in my face like I was an idiot and she showed me nothing is at all like it seems." My arms tighten around my knees. "She said he was not a cat but her familiar. She chants stuff in what I think is Latin, which I understand for some reason, but that's not important. She chanted and turned the cat into a human. It was just for a moment, but I know what I saw. The cat is not really a cat. Before she left, she made sure I knew that the same fate is waiting for me when she gets tired of either myself or my music."

When he says nothing, I dare to lift my eyes to his face. I was staring at my muddy boots while I was talking. A blank mask greets my gaze, no expression visible to tell me if he believes me or thinks I'm a nut job. My stomach caves in on itself.

"I know it sounds insane but that's the truth." I can't stop myself from blabbing. "It made me realize that I wasn't doing anyone any good by staying here. I can't help my friends when I'm a prisoner in this damn place. So, I tried to run. I was going to wait for you." He still says nothing and nerves prickle inside me. "I'm telling you the truth I was going to hide and wait. I didn't know where else to go. Who else should I tell about this? Who would actually believe me? They'll lock me up in a padded room the second I start talking about magic and cats turning into humans." Sucking in a deep breath, tears prickle my eyes. "I'm telling you the truth, I swear. I'm not crazy."

"I believe you."

"You do?"

"Yes." Tenderly, he takes my hand, his strong fingers wrapping around it as gentle as a breeze. "I told you I detest magic. I hate magic users even more. So, what happened when you entered the tunnel, apart from the pain? Tell me everything."

Chapter Sixteen

Melody

"That's all." Deflating after I recount my every step, I take strength from his touch as my mind screams, *He doesn't think I'm nuts.* I rack my brain trying to remember if I forgot anything. "She took Alto with her ..."

"I thought the cat's name was Salmon," Étienne pipes in, a small smile playing on his lips.

"I named him that because he has fish breath." Feeling stupid, I scrunch my nose up. "That's another thing, now that I think about it. When she was gloating, turning him to a human and then back to a cat, her eyes kept flashing orange, the pupils turning vertical every time she said his name."

"Witches have been getting more daring through the centuries." Étienne is glaring at the closed door so he doesn't see my mouth hanging open, my jaw unhinging at his use of centuries like he is talking about days.

"They started experimenting with things best left alone.

Magic users were once part of our world, but they slowly pulled back to hide from prying eyes so they can play games with everyone's lives." Spitting the words, he turns to me and freezes.

I'm still gaping like a fish out of water.

"Melody?" He tugs on my hand where my nails are now digging into his skin. "Are you well?"

"Centuries." I breathe the word, and he frowns like that makes me nuts. "You said centuries like you've lived through it to know."

"I'm not human." His shoulders stiffen, shutters lifting behind his eyes and closing his emotions off. "You are not human either," he tells me defensively.

"What are you? You never told me." The sweaty skin of my hand slides in his grip. I tighten my fingers because I don't want to lose the connection—as if that might force him to tell me or something.

"You didn't tell me what you are either," he points out and I wonder if I'm breaking some social decorum by asking what he is. Maybe its rude?

"That's because I have no idea if I'm human or not." Incredulous laughter bubbles up in my chest but I force it down. "I thought I was human."

"The people in that room, the ones who came to listen to your music ... they were human." The frown on his face smooths out, the silver disappearing in his gaze and leaving his eyes as blue as I remember them. "None of them left this place that night. Yet here you are, having this conversation with me."

"I didn't do anything to those people." Yanking my hand back, I jump to my feet, fear and guilt causing bile to rise at the back of my throat. "I didn't hurt anyone."

"Melody, please calm down, little one." Pushing off the

floor, he stands as well. "You didn't do anything. It was the witch. All of it."

"What are you?" If I keep thinking about all those people being dead, I'll curl up in a ball and stay like that until I die myself. So, I latch onto him for a distraction.

"A vampire." Voice flat, he stands still like I'm a firing squad aiming at his head.

"Vampire," I say, stretching the word out. With a sharp nod, he squares his shoulders.

Watching me warily, he must think I'm about to faint or laugh. Nothing can be further from the truth. What I'm doing instead is dying from embarrassment, my face burning hot and my skull numbing from it. The fact that vampires exist and that he is one of them doesn't even register in my panicked brain right now.

"Oh my God! That wasn't a dream." The words come in a rush and I cover my face with my hands. "Please tell me that was a dream or just kill me now." Spreading my fingers, I peek at him through the small gaps. "You can make it quick right? Just rip my throat out and it's done, yeah?"

"Why in fates name would I kill you." Taken aback, he even backpedals, horror twisting his pretty face.

"I begged you to kiss me." Wailing, I duck my face, wishing for the ground to open and swallow me whole.

A deep masculine chuckle slithers over my skin, sinking into every pore and turning my bones to Jello. Shivers rattle my body, my hands dropping limply to the side as I stare at him. His face lights up, his blue eyes twinkling in amusement as he watches me squirm like a five-year-old caught with a hand in the cookie jar.

"J'étais heureux d'obliger, ma petite." A smirk is playing on his lips, the amusement turning to something else in his gaze when it drops to my lips.

"What?" I sound breathless, his foreign words doing all sorts of crazy things to my insides, unable to look away.

"I was happy to oblige, little one." His deep voice sends a tremor through me.

"I'm sure you were." Murmuring under my breath, I cringe when his smile grows.

"You are not afraid of me," he points out after a while, all humor leaving his face.

I consider his comment, realizing he is right. I'm sure part of it has to do with how crazy my life is right now, but it's also him. Vampire or not, there is this aura around him that calms me. There is not a doubt in my mind that he can rip my head off or snap me in half before I have a chance to open my mouth and scream, yet those same lethal arms hold me like I'm the most precious thing in the world to him. The look on his face when he holds me to his chest tells me more than any words ever can. No one has held me like that, not even my own mother. I'm pretty sure she is not even aware I'm gone, but this stranger—this man—vampire or not, came back for me. Not just that, but here he stands holding himself stiff as a board waiting for my judgment.

Waiting for me to call him a monster.

In the last few days or however long I've been here, I learned what a monster is. Étienne, fangs or not, is as far from that as noon is from midnight. His blank face blurs when tears prickle my eyes and, unable to speak, I throw myself at him, hugging his waist like a lifeline. Pressing my face to his chest, I let the tears flow, sucking in shuddering breaths.

His startled gasp stabs me in the chest and makes me rethink this whole touchy-feely thing I'm doing around him. I've never been fond of it because I've always liked my personal bubble a bit too much, but I can't seem to keep my

Sound

hands to myself around him. Just when I start pulling away and force my arms to let go of him, his wrap around my shoulders. His body curves around mine like a shield as he presses his cheek on the top of my head.

"Melody." He sighs my name, his heart speeding up under my ear.

"Thank you for coming back for me." Holding fistfuls of the back of his shirt, I close my eyes and breathe him in.

"What good am I here if the moment you step foot in that tunnel, you stop breathing." Anger makes his deep voice sound like a growl.

"There must be a way to break the cord Seraphina tied to my chest," I tell him, not daring to look at his face while I cling to him like a spider monkey.

"What cord?" Pulling back, he glances down at me, worry dragging his eyebrows low over his eyes. "You can see her magic? She has you linked to her even now?"

"I see it only when I play. It's like a golden cord going from my chest to hers. Why are you looking at me like that?"

"Come with me." Taking my hand, he turns to the wall with determination stamped on his face.

"Oh hell no." Digging my heels in, I yank on my hand but it's like an ant trying to stop an elephant by pulling on its tail. He moves, dragging me with him. "I don't wanna die again." My screeches will definitely bring Seraphina here to investigate.

Étienne turns away from me, releasing me from his intent gaze. "I just want you to tell me what you see. I will not let you walk inside the tunnel." His nostrils flare for a second while I force myself to stop shaking. "You have no reason to trust me. Trust that I don't ever want to see you hurt."

"Okay." When he doesn't move, I nod encouragingly, although I'm dizzy just thinking about going back into that darkness.

Slowly, as if moving faster will make me bolt, he takes us to the other side of the wall. My heart is beating in my throat and bouncing off the roof of my mouth. Cold sweat dribbles between my shoulder blades as I strain my eyes to see something. Anything.

"You can't see the magic here." Not a question.

"How do you know?" Judging by the sound of his voice, I turn my face to where he is standing and blink like an owl.

"I can see your face." He doesn't laugh, but the humor is there in the sound of his voice.

We inch inside just as the sound of the lock clicks. Étienne steps back, disappearing through the wall just as Seraphina walks inside gripping Alto by the scruff of the neck, the cat hanging limp in the air. Grinning at me with some sick satisfaction, she throws the cat at me while spinning on her heel. Then she slams the door shut.

Chapter Seventeen

Étienne

Stepping back and away from Melody, I strain my ears to hear what the witch will say. Until I know what I'm dealing with and how to protect her from it, I cannot show myself. Even when my fangs are throbbing to rip the magic user's throat out. I hear the door open and Melody gasps, the soft sound coiling me up like a spring that's ready to snap and attack at a second's notice. The door closes with a thud and then nothing.

The minutes pass like hours, my bones aching from the stiffness of my muscles. No sound comes from the room, not even a breath. It could be that only a few seconds have passed, but panic that the witch snatched Melody from under my nose drains all the blood from my head. Bouncing off the balls of my feet, I fly inside the room, my knees bent and my head swiveling to find the magic user.

Melody squeaks, taking a step back and bumping her hip on the desk holding the mirror. My eyes flick to it and I see myself for the monster that her eyes can see. Snarling with my upper lip curled, my shoulders are bunched up, my fangs gleaming in the yellow light. My eyes are silver, the color swirling inside like a vortex.

"Étienne?" When she whispers my name, I finally see what she is holding in her arms. "I … I think … she killed him."

The cat hangs limp in her hands, the head and tail reaching for the floor. Taking a step closer, I stop when she bumps into the desk again. With great effort, I uncurl my lip, cracking my neck to bring some semblance of sanity to my brain. The need to protect her rides my ass so hard it takes me long moments of staring at my feet to even be able to breathe. *You don't want to scare her,* I say over and over, and finally the fangs slide back in my gums.

"I'm a horrible person," Melody says, sniffing back the tears that glisten in her eyes.

"The witch brings out the predator in me. This is all on me and not your fault." When I lift my face to look at her, she is frowning at me like I'm talking to her in French. I think I used English …

"Oh, not you." She shakes her head understanding something that I obviously do not. "She was holding Alto dead and threw him at me, but as soon as she closed the door, I couldn't stop thinking, 'thank god she didn't see my muddy broken boots.'" A tear trickles down her face. "She killed him." Lifting the cat between us, she holds it like an offering.

My head cocks to the side.

"He is still alive." The barely-there heartbeat is like butterfly wings to my ears. "Barely."

"Can you help him?" She looks around to search for something but the room has nothing we can use.

Sound

Taking the cat from her hands, I reach in with my power, merging it with the thread of life Alto still clings to. "Healing is not my strong side, but I can keep him alive until Lucien can save his life."

"Who?" Her hands hover above the cat but she doesn't touch it.

"My middle brother. He is the strongest healer I know." Yet I can't get my feet to move. I can't leave her.

The indecision must be written all over my face because Melody gives me a sad smile. Lifting on her tiptoes, she brushes a kiss on my cheek, the skin tingling in the wake of it. My gut clenches with the need to pull her into my arms.

"I'll be fine." Placing a hand on my forearm, I feel her chilled fingers through the fabric of my shirt. "Please take him to your brother. You can come back after that. It's not like I can go anywhere. I'll just wait right here."

"I can't." Shaking my head, I hate that it'll hurt her when I refuse to leave. "I need to figure out what type of an immortal you are so that we can break the spell tying you to the witch. Your life is more important."

"How can we do that?" Another fat tear slides over her cheek and lands on the edge of her jaw before splattering on my shirt, the fabric soaking it up greedily. "I have no idea what I am."

"I was hoping to snoop around here," I admit gruffly. "There must be something that can at least point us in the right direction."

"I'll do it," she offers eagerly. "I know this place better than you anyway. If I can open that door, I'll sneak around while you take Alto to your brother. Please, Étienne. If it wasn't for him, I'd have no hope of escaping. He helped by bringing you here."

I look at the creature in my hands, still alive but slipping with each second. I do not care about it; the pest has caused enough problems that I'll have to fight Lucien to get him to heal it. But as much as I hate to admit it, Melody is right. The damn cat brought me to her. That means I owe the thing a debt.

"I'll need you to stay in this room until I come back." The hope sparking in her eyes is like a knife in my chest. "No opening doors or sneaking around, Melody. She has you bound with a spell, and we don't know what she will do if she finds you lurking around the place." She nods, loosening up the knot at the back of my head.

"I'll wait." Her nails dig in the fabric of my shirt. "I won't move from that bed until you're back. Just hurry because he looks dead already."

I startle her by stealing a quick kiss. Her eyes widen and her fingers drift to her lips. With a wink, I turn and walk out of the room. My tongue sneaks out and I lick my lips, tasting the flavor of her skin on it, the pressure of the pillowy softness lingering on my mouth. The smile slips from my face as the darkness of the tunnel surrounds me before my vision flips and the colors burst into life.

"Fuck."

Cursing under my breath, I take a deep breath. I didn't have the heart to tell her that by trying to save the cat I may just kill myself. What she is not aware of, what I forget until the moment I step inside the tunnel and feel it pressing on my shoulders, is that the night is gone. The cat is barely hanging on, and I need to get back to the house while the blistering sun shines down on me.

Because it's daylight outside.

Chapter Eighteen

Melody

Okay, so I lied. I hear Étienne murmuring something from the other side of the wall while I am holding my breath waiting to hear his footsteps disappearing. I can't understand the words, but the footsteps mean he is taking Alto to be saved. More tears slide down my face as I stare at my bloody fingers. Alto's blood is covering my hands.

"What did she do to you, Alto?" I look from my hands laying in my lap to the wall where the tunnel hides.

Picking up the now-muddy shirt Étienne flicked away, I clean my hands the best I can, some dried-out blood flaking off them. That done, I unzip the muddy, broken boots and throw them under the bed, that way if Seraphina walks in she won't see them. Falling down unconscious in the tunnel soaked my clothing with mud, as well—the same mud I rubbed all over Etienne when I couldn't keep my hands to myself. It sticks to my skin, but it'll have to do for what I have in mind.

Looking around, I see the second broken heel on the floor at the foot of the bed. Picking it up, I walk to the door, eyeing the handle and the lock. As thin as it is, the heel still looks too thick to be wedged between the door and the frame. How I wish I had my credit card with me now. That would do the trick for sure.

Frustrated, I look around but see nothing that I can use. If I played the guitar, I could use the pick at least. *If you played the guitar you wouldn't have been up to your neck in shit either.* Ignoring my inner pessimist, my eyes lock on the square box of eyeshadows. Feet slapping on the floor, I snatch the compact and flick it open. I almost cry in relief when the card paper resembling a business card with instructions on how to mix the colors of the powdered shadows slides to the side.

Holding it like a holy grail, I return to the door and drop on my knees. With trembling hands, I slide the cardboard between the door and the frame, slowly guiding it down. Not wanting to rip it in two when resistance greets me, I take hold of the handle and brace on it to wiggle the door open. The pressure yanks the handle down and the door swings open, sending me on my ass gaping at the hallway, the card still stuck in my cramped fingers.

I guess due to all of Seraphina's gloating, she forgot to lock the door.

I want to scream and cry from happiness, but all I can do is force myself to slow my breathing so I don't pass out from panting. Scrambling to my feet, I hurry to the open door and stick my head out to check if the bitch is near, if she's standing here waiting for me to step out so she can kill me. An empty hallway meets my eyes.

"I can do this." Whispering under my breath, I take my first step outside the room.

Sound

Goosebumps cover my arms, but I push through the unease gnawing at my stomach. I lied to Étienne when I told him I'd wait, but only because I knew he would've let Alto die just to stay with me. Seeing a cat turn into a human and nearly die in my hands the same day makes me want to find out what I am so I can get out of here. If I find it before the vampire comes back, even better.

Vampire.

My head is spinning with everything I learned in a matter of hours. Vampires, witches, familiars ... Sliding my feet on the floor so I don't make a sound, I push those thought away. I'll think about it when I get the hell out of here. Reaching a junction where the hallway splits in two directions, I turn left instead of right. Right is where I go to perform on the nights Seraphina invites people to this place. I'm not going to think about that either.

Creeping down the unfamiliar hallway, I can't help but stick my head inside a couple of the doors in hopes that I'll find Viola or Harmony. Only empty rooms with white sheets covering the furniture meet my gaze. Wiping my sweaty palms on my yucky pants, I move forward. A headache develops at the back of my eyes from the tension in my neck and shoulders. Still, I keep moving because I'm determined to find something. A voice floats in the air from up ahead, but it's too muffled for me to hear the words. My heart kicks up like a bull against my ribs and I shuffle forward faster to follow the sound.

"... not that difficult really. The girls are too scared to be able to think, let alone try and escape." Seraphina's voice is coming from a slightly cracked door to my right. "Of course I know what I'm doing!" she snaps just as I reach the door and peek through the crack with one eye.

I didn't hear anyone else because the bitch is talking on

the phone. The room looks like an office, with one side of the desk visible to me and Seraphina stretched out on a leather chair. Her dress is bunched high on her thighs while she wiggles her toes, one ankle crossed over the other on top of the desk. Through the crack, my eyes land on shelves and shelves of thick books lining the wall.

"And how will they know that they're demigod descendants may I ask? The girls are as clueless as they are plain. There's nothing remarkable about them."

Seraphina's face reddens in anger from whatever she hears on the other side of the line. My ears are buzzing like the high-pitched horn of a passing train. Say what now? Demigod? What does that even mean? Like a child of Jesus or something? I'm not particularly religious, and neither are Viola and Harmony. If I'm one of his descendants, he will probably hit me with a bolt or something as soon as I step foot outside.

"You've heard, have you?" Seraphina sneers, straightening in her chair as her face twists in an ugly grimace that snaps me out of imagining being hit by Jesus with lightning. "Maybe you'd like to come see Melody in person, my love?" Her knuckles turn white where she grips the phone. "You haven't had time to come see me in months, but a useless girl will bring you running. I should've known. I will see you in a few days."

My heart sucker punches me in the roof of my mouth when I hear my name. Seraphina is not working alone. If whoever she's talking to says they want to meet me, I have a feeling I'll end up exactly like Alto, at least if the jealousy on her face is any indication. Gagging at the thought of some slimy bastard coming to see me, I almost swallow my tongue when Seraphina jumps off the chair and cocks her arm over her head. Plastering my back on the wall, I bite my lips so hard I taste blood to stop myself from screaming when the phone she throws smashes against the door. The impact swings the door open a little more than before.

"Yes!" Seraphina snarls, sounding deranged. "Come and see the girl Phillipe. That way I can kill you both and feast on your lives." Laughing hysterically, the chair squeaks as she swings the leather seat in a fast circle when I poke my head to the side. "A vampire and a Muse at once. That should keep me perky and young for a few centuries."

She keeps talking to herself while cackling like a lunatic. I use that time to bolt as quietly as I can through the hallway, my brain completely numb with shock. My whole body is shaking, my stomach sloshing and threatening to empty itself any second. Through a daze, I follow the hallway back to the room, white noise filling my head. *Who would've thought that someone as pleasant and pretty as Seraphina could be so evil and crazy*, I think as I cross over the open door of my room. Closing it, I lean my back on it, allowing the wood to hold my weight. Now that I'm here, my knees give out and I slide down, dropping hard on my ass and jarring my teeth. With the light streaming through the windows, the bitch almost looked angelic before her face twisted in an angry mask. Thank god Étienne is a vampire. That means he can move fast, right? He should be back any minute. I don't want to be alone all day.

Day.

"Oh my God." Pressing my hands over my mouth so I don't scream, tears stream down my face.

Étienne is a vampire. And I sent him to take Alto to his brother in the middle of the day.

Chapter Nineteen

Étienne

"What the fuck!" Lucien roars, bringing Moël running down the stairs when I shoulder my way inside the library. I can feel the skin peeling off the back of my hand hitting the polished boards with a wet, sickening sound.

"What happened to you Étienne?" The even, soft tone of Moël's voice is worse than Lucien's roar.

I must look like death worn over.

"Guéris le chat." Staggering to the desk, I place the creature on it while gently keeping contact with it. We are both barely hanging on right now, my brothers better do what I asked and heal it.

I was sticking to the shadows, using darkened alleys as much as I could. Lucky for me it's still early in the morning —not even seven-thirty yet. Had it been later I'm sure my brothers would've found the ashes of my corpse about halfway to the house.

Sound

"Were you attacked?" Moël persists, both of them ignoring the creature.

"No, I walked the daylight of my own will, brother." The horror on their faces is very telling. I want to wave at the creature but only manage a twitch of my wrist. "Now can we heal the cat?"

"I should heal you first." Lucien takes a step toward me but my glare stops him.

"I'll live. If I remove my hand the creature will die. I'm keeping it alive with my own life. Heal it."

It looks like my middle brother wants to argue, but after a long moment of shooting daggers at me through his eyes, he looms over the cat. With a disgusted look twisting his face, he places both hands on the creature and I feel his powers stretching inside it, mending everything that is broken or ripped apart. I don't know how the cat is clinging to life because so many of his bones are broken, so many muscles shredded.

Moël shoves his wrist under my nose.

"Bois." *'Drink'* He jerks his chin at me. "It'll help since Lucien might be awhile. That cursed cat looks like dogs have been chewing on it."

Keeping my mouth shut so I don't roar in pain, I take his offering by sinking my fangs in his wrist. Potent immortal blood floods my mouth and soothes the pain to a bearable level. I'm not aware of how bad of shape I'm in until I feel the relief. The longer I drink, the clearer my thoughts are. With it comes the realization that I walked in daylight to save a cat's life. Until this very moment, everything is like a fog. All I knew was that I needed to come here so Lucien could save the creature. I would've stood in the sun if Melody asked me to.

My gut drops to the floor at my feet.

"You don't look so dazed anymore," Moël murmurs as he pulls his wrist away.

"Merci." Licking my lips for the few precious drops, I nod my gratitude to my brother. "Will it live?" Avoiding staring in Moël's eyes for too long because he sees too much as it is, I turn to Lucien. I don't want them knowing that unease is eating me inside.

"I don't know how it was still alive. The fucking thing will live unless I kill it myself." Nostrils flaring, he holds both hands on the cat for a while longer while we watch. "Your turn."

"It's not healed yet." I can feel my body mending on its own, my brothers blood helping greatly. "I can wait."

"You can't wait, and the damn thing is almost as good as new. I'll get back to it after you stop looking like you'll keel over." Pushing on my shoulder, Lucien dumps me in the leather chair. All my protests are swallowed behind a clenched jaw.

Controlling my breathing and closing my eyes, I let him work. On my way here, I didn't even let myself blink because I was afraid I'd fall asleep and never wake up. What's left of my skin pulls tight where I'm fisting my hands. Pain is good. Pain means I'm still alive.

"You can talk while I work," Lucien murmurs, Moël hovering over his shoulder.

"Did you find any answers?" I watch them through heavy lids.

"There is much about the Fae, but nothing saying they need to play an instrument to access their magic." Warmth spreads through me while Lucien talks, sweat beading around his hairline. "Unless it's some ploy to hide who they are, they don't need any object for it."

"So, we still know nothing is what you're saying."

Sound

"I thought you'd bring the girl. If you had, we could've asked her. Instead, you came back with a cursed cat." I know the frustration in his voice is because of me, not Melody. Still, it irks me.

"I can't take her out of there," I tell them through clenched teeth. "She stops breathing as soon as she takes two steps out of that place."

"She is bound to the church?" Moël frowns while still looking over Lucien's shoulder.

"Or to the witch more likely." Luckily, I am watching my youngest brother as I speak. His lips pressing in a thin line and the crinkle at the corner of his eyes tells me he is holding something back. "Out with it Moël. Now is not the time for second guessing."

"I'm not sure how true what I read is." He scratches at the scar on his face. "It's a lore more than documented facts."

"Great, while I was working and having my eyes crossed from all the text I was reading, he was checking out fairy-tales," Lucien spits but I don't look away from Moël.

"It's a so-called prophecy, although it was in the ancient book of documented bloodlines that you dragged with you from the royal library." Moël keeps scratching at the scar, a quirk of his when he is deep in thought. "It speaks about the ancient gods, immortal bloodlines that were cut short a long time ago. Among the names we all know, there are three that got my attention—especially because one of them is connected with music and playing instruments. Aoide. She is the goddess, or Muse, of song, music, and tune. She prefers string instruments for her powers. I didn't mention it because it said the bloodlines are long gone. No descendants."

Stunned, I stare at my youngest brother, the feeling of

my skin growing back together forgotten. Lore or not, something inside me stirs at that name, at his words. The inner glow of Melody's eyes as she gazed at me when she took her breath tugs at my heart. Something powerful and ancient looked at me through those dark irises. I know it as well as I know my own name.

"There are descendants." I lock my gaze on Moël, and his eyes widen at whatever he sees on my face. "They were just well hidden. For a reason, I might add."

"The girl." Understanding spreads over Moël's features.

"A demigod." Lucien parks his ass on the desk and whistles low. "Do you know how powerful and potent her immortal blood is? We can level whole cities on it alone."

"No one touches her blood." One second I am sitting on the chair, and the next I have Lucien pinned by the throat on my desk. "Are we clear?"

"She really is your mate." Lucien wheezes, somehow managing to laugh like the asshole he is even when I'm choking him. "Stay away from the muse, got it brother."

"This is not funny." Snarling, I push him hard, banging his head on the desk before I release him. "I need to see that text Moël. I don't think I can leave the house until nightfall. One more stroll through daylight might be my undoing."

"Demigod or not, I still don't understand how can she be a vampire's mate." Rubbing his neck, Lucien lifts on one elbow but stays sprawled on my desk. "Moël?" My head snaps to my younger brother at the panic on Lucien's face.

"Tu penses que c'est vrai?" All the blood is drained from Moël's face, the scar standing out more prominent against his skin as he drops in the closest chair he can find. "The stories father used to tell us when we were young? You think they are true?"

"Father was telling made up shit when he was blood-drunk. We all know that." Dismissing him with a wave of his hand, Lucien keeps rubbing at his neck.

"Which story are you referring to?" I know very well what he is talking about because the moment he starts talking about the lore, my father's words were floating through my brain. I just want him to say it.

"That mother was a descendant of a muse?" His Adam's apple bobs up and down before he can speak again. "He always said that our love for learning the old ways was because she was a descended of Clio, the muse of history. Could that be the reason why the girl is your mate?"

"Fuck." Even Lucien looks stricken now. My middle brother finally catching up with the rest of us. "I forgot about that." He scrubs a hand over his face roughly. He will be scrubbing more by the time I'm done talking.

"There are two more females held in that church."

All the oxygen is sucked out of the room.

You can hear a pin drop.

"He knew." Moël nods slowly as he puts the pieces together just as I already did. "He knew whatever the prophecy, it was about to start and that he was going to die. That's why a week before he was killed he made each of us promise to stick together, no matter what happens. He made us give a blood oath."

"Quelles sont les chances?" Lucien sounds like he is about to faint.

"Yeah." I chuckle humorlessly. "What are the odds?"

Chapter Twenty

Melody

This is the longest day of my life.

At one point, I almost go out to stir some shit up so Seraphina comes here. Even dealing with her and her sadistic cruelty is better than counting the milliseconds, holding my breath, and waiting to see if Étienne will come back or if I sent him to his death. If he does come ... No! *When* he comes back, I'm going to scratch his eyes out for listening to me. I've already chewed through all the skin around my nails while staring at the wall unblinking. My butt is going numb, and every time I shift ants crawl up and down through my legs.

Still, I don't dare move.

When the scrape of a rock comes from behind the wall, my whole body clenches. I've never seen a more beautiful sight than his blond head poking through, his silvery gaze locking on mine the same second.

"Melody." The small smile sends a ping through my

Sound

chest, the lilt he puts to my name tracing a shiver up my spine.

Whimpering, I scramble to my feet and, losing my footing, pitch forward. Moving fast, he snatches my flailing body in his arms, the warmth from his chest bringing sensation back to my numb limbs.

"What has happened, little one." Smoothing the hair off my face, he searches my tear-smudged face. "I promised I would be back. The cat lives." He grins proudly. With that my brain gets back online.

I slap him.

"Melody?" Rearing back, his hand presses on his cheek, which is swollen from my smack.

"You could've died you idiot!" Shoving him away, I struggle out of his grip. "It was daylight outside!" Stabbing a finger angrily at the wall, I glare at him. Then a thought occurs to me. "Can you walk in the day? All the movies I've seen show vampires turning to ash if they are out in the daylight."

"That's one thing humans got right." His lips twitch in a barely-restrained smile.

"What were you thinking?"

"I wasn't."

"You should've ... wait, what?"

"I wasn't thinking." Taking my hand, he pulls me back in his arms. "I just wanted to do anything you asked of me."

"You know that's insane right?" All the fear for his life hits me at once and I sag in his arms. "You could've died. What kind of a vampire are you if a girl tells you to go out in the sun and you listen." The fact that I was scared I'd never see him again is not lost on me, but I'll dwell on that later.

"I was not asked by just any girl, now was I?" he says it

softly, the deep tone of his voice melting me in his embrace. "I know what you are."

"Yeah, so do I." Blurting the words out like an idiot, I feel all gooey inside.

"How?" Jerking back, he eyes me with suspicion, and I want to kick myself.

"I was worried about you and couldn't sit still so I might've lurked around the hallways," I tell him sheepishly, biting on my lip. His gaze turns smoldering as he zeroes in where my teeth are sewing my skin. "I heard Seraphina talking to someone on the phone. She mentioned demigods and descendants of a Muse." Anger bubbles up when I think about it again. "Whoever she was talking to is coming in a few days. He wants to see me, not Vi or Harmony. I don't know why." Étienne is staring at my mouth like he's mesmerized, and I try not to swoon. "She called him Phillipe," I murmur, watching his face just as mesmerized.

"What?" He jumps back like I've slapped him and breaks the moment.

"She called him Phillipe." Shaking my head to clear it, I watch his face cloud over with rage. "Étienne?"

"Did she speak French?"

"No. Was she supposed to? What's going on?" All the warmth I got back in my bones disappears from the murder written all over his face. "She is wrong right? It's insane that I'm a descendant of Jesus."

"Jesus," The deadpan way he says it pisses me off.

"She said demigod, Étienne." Widening my eyes, I speak slowly for his scrambled brain. Maybe the sun did a number on him. "Jesus is a god."

His eyes flick through mine before he throws back his head and lets out a deep, masculine laugh that fills the room.

Sound

Panicking, I jump at him and slap a hand over his mouth because I'm afraid Seraphina will hear him and come running. He didn't say he knows how to fight her, just that he knows what I am. Now he is laughing at me, the jerk.

"Be quiet!" Hissing, I watch mirth dancing in his eyes that have gone back to pools of endless blue. "The sun made you a little stupid, didn't it?"

Shaking his head like I'm a two-year-old, he pulls at my fingers that are glued on his face like an octopus. Placing a soft kiss at the center of my palm, he smooths my hand at the center of his chest. His heart beats strong and steady under my skin, confirming yet again that somehow, he survived being out in the day.

"You are a descendant of a god, making you a demigod yes." Another kiss whispers, this time on my forehead. "Your bloodline comes from one of the three Muse's, Melody. That is why you feel so connected to your violin. Through your instrument, your powers are manifesting." The next kiss is on my eyelid.

"I've never heard of a Muse god." Keeping my eyes closed, I'm not sure I say it out loud or in my head. Butterflies are alive in my lower belly and they are making me dizzy. "Is it evil?"

"Whatever makes you think it's evil?" Cupping my face, the touch of his skin flutters my eyelids open.

"My music ... it hurts people." The words come out choked up.

"Your music feeds passion, little one. You do not hurt people, the witch stealing your life energy does." Something scary flashes in the depths of his eyes but it's gone the next second. "We need to break the bond."

"You know how to break the golden rope?" Hope

blooms in my chest and smothers the butterflies. "I can get out of here without dying?"

Étienne watches me carefully and nods slowly. "Yes, I need to mark you." At my frown, he explains more. "When I mark you, a bond will form between us. It'll be stronger than any magic a witch can weave. That will free you from this cursed place."

"So, you'll have to mark Vi and Harmony to get them out, too?" For some reason that idea makes me see red. I've never been the jealous type, but if my friends were here I think I would've attacked them. Étienne looks smug, like he just won the lotto or something. I can attack him instead of my friends.

"No, I cannot mark your friends." Chuckling, he smooths my scrunched-up forehead with the pad of his thumb. "I can only mark one female for as long as I live. You. I can only mark you."

A goofy smile spreads over my face until my stupefied brain kicks in. "There is a catch, isn't there." My eyes narrow on his pretty face. It's always the pretty ones that try to manipulate you, isn't it? "You are not telling me the whole thing."

"My brothers will come back to get your friends away from here. If what I know is right, they'll be able to mark them as well." His gaze flicks to the vein throbbing in my neck and my heart starts galloping harder against my ribs.

"Why can you only mark me?"

All the amusement and joking washes off his face. The serious look in his gaze sends a jolt of something through me that makes me hold my breath. The gravity of whatever he is about to say presses on me even before I hear the words.

"Because you are my mate." His chest fills with so much

air I'm almost lifted off him. A deep sigh comes out, the air stirring the hair around my face. "You are the day to my night, the light to my darkness, and the missing part of my soul. Will you allow me the honor to mark you as mine?"

The lump in my throat is choking me and I can barely breathe. His face is swimming from the tears overfilling my eyes. Somewhere along the way in this nightmare, I started caring for him. No matter how much everything inside me is screaming to say yes, I still don't know him well enough to get the words out of my mouth.

Hurt flashes in his blue gaze and I want to do everything I can to make it go away. Still, the tongue is glued to the roof of my mouth and no words come out. That's when I hear it. The faint click cluck of heels coming from behind the closed door. The blood curdles in my veins when Étienne moves, but instead of turning to the wall, he faces the closed door while pushing me behind his back.

"Yes!" I almost scream the word, yanking on his shoulder so he can face me. "Mark me." Bearing my neck, I tilt my head as far as it'll go. "Mark me, damn you. I'll be your mate. Hurry!"

"Are you sure?" A frown is pulling on his forehead. "This is for eternity, Melody. There is no going back from it. No escape."

The click cluck, albeit slow, is coming closer. The bitch knows when I can hear her, and she loves dragging things on to torment me. But Étienne deserves better than me being mute one second and forcing him to mark me the next.

"I don't want to escape from you." I let him see the truth in my eyes as I crane my neck to look at him. "I would've liked to know you better before this but every story worth reading has a commonality. Destiny waits on no one to make up their mind. Mark me, please. We will figure everything else out together."

I'm shocked to realize I mean every word that comes out of my mouth. I've never been a risk taker, or adventurist making haste decisions, but this feels right on a soul-deep level. The truth must be loud and clear because Étienne gathers me in his arms and sinks his fangs in the skin of my neck.

Heat spreads through my body and an orgasm hits me out of nowhere, but I can't even make a sound. His lips are fused on my skin, his wet tongue gliding over it. Condensed air punches the center of my chest. It makes me feel like my soul is being ripped apart when the thread connecting me to Seraphina breaks apart, but warmth soothes it the next second and I feel Étienne, the happiness that he is trying to hide so he doesn't freak me out, and his amazement when he feels me as well. It feels natural.

It feels right.

A furious scream rattles the wall around us. A force like a tsunami rips the door off its hinges and flings it at our heads. Seraphina's anger is like a living thing trying to choke the life out of us. Étienne lifts his head and gives me such a boyish smile I turn into a puddle even while I'm almost peeing my pants from the magic swirling around us. I can hear Seraphina running in the hallway.

"Let's get out of here." Scooping me up in his arms, he heads for the wall.

"No wait, my violin."

"That's not your violin. I took your instrument when you dropped it the night I found you." Not slowing down, we melt through the wall just as Seraphina screams again in rage.

Sound

"Hold on tight," Étienne tells me, and I tuck my face in the crook of his neck. "Let's go home."

Clinging to him while he moves like the wind, I can't help but pray that Vi and Harmony don't have to pay for my escape. I promise them silently that I'll do everything to send Étienne's brothers to save them.

"Just hold on," I whisper to them both, but I know they'll never hear me.

Chapter Twenty-One

Étienne

"There it is again. It's looking at me." Melody pokes me in the ribs while clutching the back of my shirt in a tight fist. I do my best to hold back the smile trying to emerge while she uses my back as her hiding place.

"I'm not sure my brother appreciates you referring to him as an 'it,' little one." Lucien's glare turns frosty when he swings his gaze from my mate to me. "Although, I can see why you decided to refer to him as such." The smile that threatened earlier finally stretches my lips at Lucien's reaction.

"How are you doing this?" Melody tugs on my shirt until I look at her over my shoulder. "How is your reflection in the mirror acting independently like it's a living thing. Is it a vampire mojo thingy you can do?"

With a deep sigh, I squeeze the bridge of my nose between a thumb and a forefinger, debating if I should knock my brother on his ass for acting like an idiot. I had to dress appropriately in my attempt to rescue Melody, so I took his clothing since he favors black over anything else. Bringing my still-fearful and stressed-out mate home, where he decided to block our path in the hallway dressed exactly the same and just stare at her like he's never set his eyes on a female before without saying a word, didn't help matters either. The last twenty minutes I've been trying to convince her that he is not my reflection in a mirror.

"Si tu ne parles pas, je te botterai le cul et elle verra que tu peux saigner." Threatening him with violence does the trick, especially after I remind him that I *can* and *will* make him bleed.

"C'est une toute petite chose." Cocking his head to the side, he moves closer until Melody gasps and ducks behind my back. "I was telling my brother that you are very petite. Small. Not what I expected from a demigod." His grin uncovers the tips of his fangs, and no amount of anger on my part will wipe it out.

"You didn't tell me you had a twin." Melody sounds upset as she steps out and reveals herself to my brother. "That would've saved me a lot of embarrassment," she mutters under her breath before offering Lucien a bright smile that looks strained on her tear-smeared face.

"Hello." Giving him a little wave, she turns from him to me expectantly. "Ummm ... I don't know which one you are, or your name for that matter. So, yeah ... hi." With a tiny shrug of one shoulder, her hands flatten over her thighs and she brushes the pants she is wearing as if trying to clean them.

"That's Lucien." I finally make the interdiction. "My middle brother ..." my voice trails off when Melody gasps and practically jumps at my brother, wrapping both arms around his waist.

Nothing can prevent the feral growl that rips from my chest. Lucien's arms shoot out to the sides, his palms up in surrender. He can clearly see that I'm a second away from attacking him like he is my worst enemy. The tension in the hallway is so thick I can barely take a breath, while my mate obliviously snuggles closer to my brother's chest muttering something over and over under her breath. With great effort, I silence the thundering in my ears so I can hear her words.

"I did not touch her." Lucien grinds the words between clenched teeth, his arms still up in the air. He is also holding his breath in such a way it is as if he thinks if he caves his chest in he can distance himself from her. "Do be a good male and peel her off me if you would be so kind, brother."

"Thank you, thank you. Thank you so much …" Melody keeps muttering breathlessly while clinging to him for dear life. "I'm so sorry I called you an 'it.' I'm sorry, truly sorry …"

With a frown, my eyes dart from my mate to my brother and I see his gaze slowly lower to the top of her head. When he hears what she is saying to him, one of Lucien's eyebrows cocks up before he swings his eyes to my face, the question clear to see in his wide orbs. Melody keeps apologizing and thanking him at the same time, and that makes me realize why she has acted this way.

"I told her that you saved the cat's life," I spit the words at Lucien like he's done something wrong, which angers me even more. I shouldn't be acting like this. Seeing her wrapped around my brother makes me want to strangle the damn cat just so I can bring it back to life for her.

"Étienne." The warning is clear in Lucien's voice, so I stride to him and tug Melody gently until she reluctantly releases her hold.

Sound

"Come, little one." Tucking her under my arm, warmth spreads through me when she snuggles there like she belongs nowhere else. "My brother is humbled by your gratitude. Let us sit. You are barely standing on your feet." Ignoring the incredulous look on Lucien's face, I guide her to the living room. Her head swivels left and right as she tries to see everything she is passing.

For the first time, I wish I could get inside her head to see what she is seeing. Does she like my home? Will she want to stay or leave me? My heart skips a beat. I've never cared at all one way or another. I've always tried to make this place we're stuck in resemble the home we left behind, at least as much as I can. Is it too foreign for my mate? She grew up as a human, living her life in modern times while I've been stuck in the past hoping to right wrongs. Will I lose her before I have a chance to have her? With questions weighing on my heart, I lower her gently on the large lounge, her tiny frame almost disappearing in the cumbersome thing. With a frown pulling on my brows, I glare at the damn thing. Why in all the world did we get the antique-carved piece, and how long has it been here?

"Ethan?" Melody's soft, fearful voice brings me out of my turbulent thoughts, and I realize I've been growling.

"I apologize, little one." Crestfallen at my reaction, I take a step away from her so she doesn't fear me. "I was wondering when we got this hideous thing you are sitting on. I don't remember it being this horrible …"

Lucien's snickering makes me trail off, and I can scowl at him. Undisturbed, my brother saunters into the room grinning from ear to ear before he throws himself on one of the chairs, sprawling across it like an ass. Flinging one arm over the back of the armchair and a leg over one armrest, he keeps chuckling and shaking his head.

"I don't get it." Melody squirms on the large cushion, her eyes darting between Lucien and I.

"Ah, but I do, little demigod." Lucien fully guffaws at my scolding glare. "And I must say I'm looking forward to the upcoming days. You see"—Leaning forward, he points at Melody with one finger, his grin turning cunning enough to raise the hairs on the back of my neck. "I've never met anyone that can ruffle my brother's feathers like this. And I'm planning to have a front seat for this drama. If I knew he would turn into an old lady fretting over furniture and whatnot, I would've snatched you that first night at the club."

The moment the last words were out of his mouth he realizes his mistake, just as I do. All the blood drains from Melody's face and I feel the terror coursing through her veins from the newly formed bond we have. Not an hour ago I saved her from a fate where she was snatched from her life and held against her will, and my brother had to stupidly open his damn mouth and say something idiotic to remind her of that. Before I can turn on him and rip his throat out, he jumps out of the chair and backs up until his spine is pressed against the large window behind him.

"I did not mean it that way. None of us will do anything against anyone's will, little demigod. I meant it as a joke, albeit not a very funny one given the circumstances ..." With a groan, he rubs his hand over the top of his head in frustration, messing his hair so much that it's sticking up all over the place. "If you don't know my brother that well, I should tell you he has a stick up his ass. Someone leaving him fretting like an old maid is not something we see often. That is all I was trying to say ... it came out wrong."

Fists balled at my sides, I take a step toward him only to stop in my tracks when a giggle bursts from Melody's lips. A snort follows, and Lucien and I slowly turn to see the little female doing her best not to laugh in our face. Her face is red, and she's biting her lips, her nostrils flaring while chuckles and snorts come from her throat in small increments. Faking a cough, she tries to cover up her reaction but eventually gives up and peals of laughter fill the room while her hands cover her mouth in a useless attempt to prevent them.

I've never heard a more beautiful sound.

Both Lucien and I sway toward her before we catch ourselves and shake our heads to clear them. I purposely ignore the pointed look Lucien gives me, the unease of our reaction all but forgotten when her face brightens with a smile. Even aware that our reaction is not normal, both of us smile at her, joining in the lighthearted feeling outside of our control.

"You should see yourselves." Melody giggles, wiping the tears from the corners of her eyes. "It's like watching two bears ready to eat you one second and apologizing for having big teeth the next." More laughter follows before she can speak again. "This is my life now. Witches that hold me captive with magic, cats that turn into humans, and vampires apologizing for having uncomfortable furniture." All humor leaves her face, and she looks at me with a somber expression. "I've lost my mind, haven't I? This whole thing is in my head, isn't it? I'm on psychotic drugs in some white-padded room while I'm rocking myself back and forth, aren't I?" More laughter explodes from her as she shakes her head.

The worry clawing at my insides is the same worry I see on Lucien's face. Maybe it was too much to hope that she would take everything in stride. That she would accept everything for what it is.. Being outside of that cursed place and away from the magic has finally broken her mind. Panic churns in my gut, and it leaves me frozen. I have no idea what to do. *She is your mate,* a voice inside me whispers. *You can soothe her and calm her. You can piece her back together if she breaks.*

I'm not sure if that's true, but I'm willing to try anything to keep my mate well.

Chapter Twenty-Two

Melody

"Bring the violin," Étienne tells his brother without looking away from me.

I'm doing my best to stop laughing, but I can't. Tears run unchecked down my face. My whole body is trembling inside, and my blood is running cold through my veins. Filling my lungs with short gasps of air, the fact that I'm aware I'm having a panic attack doesn't help stop it. It actually makes it worse. It's like I can't control my reactions and it's making me hyperventilate. The only thing holding me together and not forcing me burst at the seams is keeping my eyes locked on Étienne's face, so I cling to that like a lifeline.

"I'm not sure it's a good idea with this particular female brother, mate or not." Lucien's unease might be comical if not for the fact that I'm falling apart in front of their eyes. The stoic, mean-looking copy of Étienne seems almost as panicked as I am.

"Do it." The order is unmistakable in the deep voice passing the lips that kissed me tenderly not long ago, and Lucien obeys, though he mutters many foreign words I don't understand under his nose.

"Melody, look at me." Étienne inches closer like he is approaching a wounded animal. He drops on his knees when he is a couple of feet away to put us at eye level, which I'm thankful for since I don't have to crane my neck to meet his gaze. Taking my cold fingers in his large palm, his thumb rubs soothing small circles at the back of my hand. "You are safe here, little one. I won't let anyone or anything harm you. I swear it on my life. Just breathe."

"You are a vampire and I'm a demigod," I stupidly tell him, giggling through every word. I'm very aware how unhinged I sound, but there's no help for it at the moment. "And magic exists that traps people, feeds off their life, and makes them do things they're not aware of." My free hand waves jerkily in the air as if the room is full of magic. It's not. I should know since I don't feel like something is trying to crawl under my skin and peel off my bones.

"That we are," he tells me, a small smile playing at the corners of his mouth. The tenderness in his blue eyes forms a lump in my throat, the intensity choking me. "And what a pair we are, ma petite. Believe me when I say I will level this continent all the way to Hell before I allow anyone to get near you again." Bringing my numb fingers to his face, he peppers soft kisses on my knuckles. "Just breathe. Everything will be fine." His lips graze my skin with each word warming the ice that spreads inside me.

"Here it is." Lucien walks in holding my violin in a tight fist as if he wants nothing more than to break it into tiny splinters. I can't blame him for it since I know what me

Sound

playing the instrument can do. "I still think it isn't a good idea, but you never listen to me anyway." He shoves the violin under Étienne's face, wiggling it to encourage him to take it faster.

"Merci." Étienne's hand takes the instrument, and he doesn't look at his brother once as he lowers it across his thighs where he is still kneeling in front of me. "I think I know what will calm you, little one, but I do need my other hand as well." Tilting his chin, he points at the hand I'm still clutching like a drowning man clinging to a straw.

I release him reluctantly, uncurling my fingers with great effort one by one. Swallowing thickly, I ball my fist and tuck it under my leg so I don't latch onto him again. I've never been a clingy person, but right now I feel like the only thing that can stop me from losing my mind is if I crawl under his skin so I can hide from everything. His features soften as if he knows exactly how I feel, and my face burns in embarrassment. *Way to go, Melody. Show him why he doesn't want anything to do with you.* My inner critic helps me keep my hands away from the handsome man kneeling at my feet. Lucien stands until he is looming above us with his arms crossed across his chest like a guardian, and for some reason it makes me feel better knowing he will protect his brother. Especially if Étienne wants me to play for him.

My jaw drops to my chest when Étienne swings the violin gracefully to his shoulder and winks at me just before lowering the bow to the strings. My heart kicks against my ribs when he closes his eyes, his thick, long lashes hiding his stark blue orbs from my view as he starts playing. It's slow at first, as if he is unsure of what he is doing, but soon enough a soothing, beautiful melody I've never heard before wraps around me like an embrace. Still gaping, I can't take my eyes away from his graceful fingers as they move across the strings, and before I know it, my heartbeat is even and I'm mesmerized all over by this mysterious man that has barged into my life out of nowhere. The music stops way too soon, and he opens his eyes slowly, a smile stretching his kissable lips when he sees me staring at him like I'm looking at an alien.

"I take it I didn't do bad." Lowering the violin, his head tilts slightly to the side and I realize he is listening to my heartbeat. How I know this is beyond me, but I'm sure of it, just as sure as I am that my name is Melody. "It's been a while since I've played any instrument."

"You can play the violin." Pointing out the obvious, I blink at him because I'm still stunned at what I just heard.

"A little." Glancing away as if ashamed, he clears his throat before focusing on me again. "You feel better now, no?" When I just nod mutely, his lashes lower halfway to hide the emotions swirling in his blue eyes. "I had a feeling music will soothe you like nothing else. It's in your blood. It's what you are …"

"Thank you." There is a lot I want to say, but with Lucien still staring down at us like he is, all I can do is fidget on the large couch, the hard cushion making my butt go numb. "And I'm sorry for going a little nuts there for a moment. We have more important things to worry about than me losing my mind right now." Étienne frowns disapprovingly at this, but I can finally think clearly again, and my friends being left in Seraphina's clutches is all I can think about.

"You need to rest, Melody." Étienne places the violin on the floor, all tenderness gone from the tone of his voice. "I promised I'd save your friends, and I will, but you are not going anywhere near that place again."

Sound

"And who's going to stop me?" Anger like a tidal wave rushes through me when his eyebrows dip low over his eyes, his frown bunching his forehead. "I'm coming with you when you go to get them."

"Absolutely not." Étienne's hand slices the air in front of him with finality.

"You are not my mother." Hissing at him, I jump to my feet. "I don't need your help; I'll just call the police. They'll get Vi and Harmony out of there." I'm well aware that none of my words are true, but my stubbornness doesn't allow me to back down. With everything I know now, the police will probably lock me up the minute I open my mouth and start talking about witches and magic.

"Humans will not even find the cursed place, female. And you are not going anywhere near that magic user again." Uncurling to his full height, he stands up too. I forgot how tall he is until I crane my neck to keep eye contact and a king forms almost immediately. "Are you trying to make this more difficult than it needs to be?"

"How dare you!" Unable to stop myself, I scream at him. Warmth spreads through my arms and legs, and I take a step toward him despite my brain screaming at me to stop. A force inside me awakens, and rage at the fact that he dares to command me as if he is superior takes over. "I will do as I want, and you can't tell me otherwise."

"Melody." My name is a warning and a plea, and when he glances at me, confusion clouds his perfect features.

"This I will enjoy watching." Lucien chuckles, plopping on the chair he was sitting on earlier, all guarding and protecting his brother from me forgotten. "Carry on, don't mind me."

"None of you are going anywhere if what I found is

correct." A third guy walks in looking exactly like Étienne and Lucien, apart from the scar on his face.

Blinking rapidly, I look from one to the other, and then to the third. My brain has finally had enough exercise with all the impossible things going on. The eyes roll to the back of my head and I drop on the stupid couch.

Chapter Twenty-Three

Étienne

"The two of you need to stop acting like uncivilized peasants." My voice snaps like a whip between the three of us as I arrange Melody's limbs so she is more comfortable on the lounge.

"I didn't mean to scare the female." Moël shrugs nonchalantly, his hand raising to the scar on his face before he catches himself dropping it to his side. Guilt gnaws at me, but I push it away somehow. He should know better. "So, this is her?" Inching closer, he curiously peers at my mate over my shoulder.

"This is Melody, yes." Brushing the strands of curled hair from her face, my fingers linger there longer than necessary. The feel of her skin is like silk under my touch, and I can't stop myself from brushing it with my hand. "My mate."

No matter how many times I say it, it still sounds incredible and surreal to my ears. A mate. What are the odds? My youngest brother's hum brings me back from the warmth I am drowning in from that thought.

"About that, brother ... and take what I'm saying with a grain of salt." Blowing out a heavy sigh, Moël moves around the low table to take the second armchair. He leans forward and steeples his fingers with forearms resting on his knees, a somber look in his eyes that's so unlike his usual carefree attitude. "I went researching the Muses and everything else I can find about them. What I found"—His pause does not sit well with me, and I feel myself stiffening at the reluctance I see in him—"is not necessarily a bad thing, but there is a catch to it. As there always is when one decides to play with gods and their descendants."

"What does that mean?" Lucien growls, my own frustration spiking at the harshly spoken words. "Can you just say it without all the dramatic pauses and the rest of the bullshit. We are not at court, so you have no one to impress, brother."

"I wasn't doing dramatic ..." Huffing in annoyance, he looks at me and ignores the glare Lucien gives him. "The problem is, I don't know how true what I found is. According to one of the old texts that you must've dragged with us from Paris, a pact was made between a magic user and the Muses. They offered their descendants as a weapon against us." His gaze swings to Melody and his jaw flexes for a long moment.

Lucien snarls and lifts off his chair, but my raised hand stops him halfway up. Our eyes lock in a silent battle of wills, and as unheard of as it may seem, I make sure he sees clearly that I will kill him if he tries to harm my mate. My mind accepts the possibility of what Moël is saying. When I saw her so mellow and so unlike herself while she was under the influence of the drugs the witch gave her, the same thought had occurred to me. But something deeper nags at my heart telling me it can't be true. I cannot envision Melody harming anyone. Not purposely. The female wanted to trade her life to protect the damn cat for fate's sake.

"What else did you find, Moël?" Keeping my gaze on Lucien, I don't even dare blink because my power is scratching under my skin to be unleashed. Brother or not, if he moves one finger, all Hell will break loose.

"It also said that the only way to avoid certain death is to win the Muse's heart. A heart none of them are willing to offer to one of our kind. It must be something that happened in the old days between a Muse and one of ours, something to force gods to make pacts with magic wielders." From the corner of my eye, I see him scratching at the scar on his face, his last words murmured as if he is talking to himself instead of us. "She doesn't look very dangerous to me." He sounds shocked as he keeps staring at my mate.

"Il faut se méfier de l'eau qui dort." Lucien grumbles, wisely lowering his ass back in the chair.

"What did he say?" Melody's raspy voice is like a caress to my ears.

"Do not trust calm waters," Moël answers her question by translating in English, the curiosity still visible on his face. "I'm Moël. The best looking one in the family." His devilish grin is lost on my mate.

"Hi." With a tight press of her lips, she tries to smile at him, though her attempt is unsuccessful. "I'm Melody, and I have no intention of killing anyone." Wiggling, she pushes my hands away to sit up cross-legged on the lounge, and then she faces both my brothers. "I didn't hear everything you said, but I heard the important part." She keeps watching them like she is trying to avoid my gaze, which opens a chasm in my chest. "I'm well aware of what happens when I play my violin, so I can put your mind at ease by telling you I decided to never play again as long as I live. Without my music, I'm just a regular, harmless human."

Moël's eyebrows crawl up his forehead while Lucien bursts out laughing without humor, and that pisses me off. "That's a big promise for someone who can kill the only heirs to the French throne, little demigod." My middle brother sneers and the fangs slide from my gums. "Your kind is well known for manipulation and trickery. You will not fool me like you did my brother."

"Lucien, that's enough!" The windows rattle from my roar, but none of them blink an eye, including Melody.

"I can't say you are lying," she tells my brother evenly, my anger not bothering her one bit. "You see, I had no idea what I was until today. Or was it yesterday? I have no clue since I have no idea how long I was held captive. I don't even know what day it is. So, you could be right. That's why I will leave and never bother any of you again. I'll find a way to save my friends alone."

"Like hell you will leave. Melody ..." My blood turns to ice at her words, but when she turns her dark, tear-filled eyes on me, the words I want to say get stuck in my throat and I can't get any of them out.

"No, Étienne. Thank you for saving me and giving me the opportunity to do the same for Vi and Harmony, but your brother is right. I don't belong here." One fat tear trickles down her face, and it's like a dagger to my heart. "I don't belong around anyone that I can harm, for that matter."

"I could be wrong," Moël offers, but Melody is already shaking her head.

"You could also be right." A sad smile tilts her lips up. "Are you willing to chance it? Because I'm not. That's not how I want to show gratitude for saving my life."

I'm frozen in place when she stands, glancing around the room as if trying to remember it because she never plans on returning here. The chasm in my chest spreads wider, the gaping hole shredding my insides with a pain I've never felt before. Melody shuffles her feet as if expecting me to stop her, but I can't move or open my mouth to save my life. Panic grips me in its clutches when she takes the first step to lead her away from me. Something primal rears its head, and it takes over all rational thoughts. My body jerks off the lounge where I'm perched.

"You will not walk away from me." I don't recognize my own voice, and apparently neither does Melody because she jumps away with wide eyes.

"Étienne." The warning in Moël's voice only angers me more. Melody, on the other hand is a different story.

"Oh, yeah?" Her hip cocks and she slams a fist on it, defiance flashing in her brown eyes. "And what are you going to do about it? Force me to stay?"

"That's exactly what I'm going to do if you take one more step, Melody. Do not test me." In the back of my mind, I know I'm making things worse and I should reason with her, but the predator in me is awake and will tear this house down to prevent his mate from leaving.

The feisty female I saw in the club what feels like lifetimes ago smiles at me, a dare to stop her as clear as a sunshine on her face. Melody takes one purposeful step away from me, her chin jutting out stubbornly. My vision bathes in red and my shoulders hunch, readying my body to pounce on her. Her eyes widen for a second before something dark comes flying at my head from the open door.

Twisting around, I snatch it in the air and fling it at the wall away from me. Melody shrieks so loud my eardrums almost burst from the sound, and it takes a moment for what she screamed to actually penetrate my clouded brain.

"No! Salmon!" is what my mate screamed just a second before the damn cat slammed into the wall falling limp on the floor.

"Fuck!" The word is a hiss that's jumbled through my fangs.

Chapter Twenty-Four

Melody

Horror like I've never felt before strangles any other words that are trying to push through my mouth. Hearing that I'm not just unwanted but also feared in the only place I have felt safe for the first time in what feels like forever is the final straw in this entire nightmare. I mean, what kind of monster do you need to be for vampires to be afraid? I should've stayed in my prison and let Seraphina drain my life. Being turned into a cat is better than having this empty, painful feeling overtaking my chest cavity.

"Don't!" My choked cry stops Étienne when he takes a step closer to me.

What do I even know about him?

Trapped in that damn place, I let my emotions and fear guide my actions, following and trusting him blindly. But isn't that what got me in this whole mess in the first place? Latching onto the first person who can help me, I didn't think things through. Now here he is, fangs bared, snarling and threatening me while hurting Salmon without a care in the world. My feet shuffle back until I'm closer to the open door. All three of them track me with their eyes, eerily still like statues in a horror movie where only eyes follow your movements. Although my heart is thundering in my ears, I still slide further away from them in a futile attempt to get the hell out of here. *You are so stupid, Melody. This is what you get for being a freak.* Tears keep rolling down my cheeks unchecked, but I couldn't care less if they see me cry. Still, my trembling fingers brush them away to clear my blurry vision. As if that will make things better. If I can see them, they won't hurt me. Rigghhtt ...

"I believe what Melody needs is some time to gather her thoughts." The last one who walked in, the one with the scar, says conversationally, like he didn't just announce to everyone in the room that I'm a monster.

Everything in me wants to ask if Salmon is okay, but survival is more important to me now. I don't want any part of this anymore. Cats that turn into humans, magic, witches, vampires ... they can all go to hell. I just want to run and keep running for eternity if I have to, or until I get my sanity and life back. A life before music. A life before I stupidly started having feelings for a guy I saw only once—and a few minutes at that—before he showed up to save the day. One hell of a coincidence if you ask me. Something that didn't occur to me until just now. With clenched fists, I inch closer to the door, my eyes darting between the three men in the room with me.

"Melody ..." Étienne sighs and brushes a hand roughly over his face. "Toutes mes excuses, chère petite." Clenching his chiseled jaw, he groans as if pained. "I apologize is what

Sound

I tried to say." More words in French follow, and I don't need to understand them to know he is cursing up a storm. "Emotions are running high at the moment, so let us all calm down and talk this through. This is one of the reasons I detest magic. Whenever magic gets involved, no one acts like themselves and we all turn on each other."

"Umm, no. I'm good, actually." His eyes narrow when I slide further away, and I'm almost at the open door now. "No need to talk anything through. Look at us." Pointing with a trembling finger, I wave my hand between us, first pointing at my chest. "I'm calm, he is calm, he is calm too, and you are practically an epitome of calmness yourself, sir. All is good in da hood. I'll just be on my way—"

"You can't leave, Melody," he tells me evenly, while the other two are watching us like they are at a tennis match.

"Of course I can. Watch me, I'll just put one foot in front of the other and I'll be out of here before you say tamale." Which is a lie since I have no idea where the damn front door is.

"You can't leave because I marked you, mon amour. Remember that? You agreed and urged me to do it." The intensity in his blue eyes makes my knees wobble, so I lock them in case I crumble on the floor in a heap like some idiot.

"I can't be the only girl you bit, Étienne. You might be the first vampire I've seen, but I'm not stupid. Who knows how many had you chewing on their neck, and I don't see any girls prancing around this place." Dread spreads through me before I'm done talking. "Oh my God, do you have them locked up somewhere?"

"Melody." He rubs his forehead as if he is getting a headache, but I'm beside myself from the thought.

"Don't you *Melody* me you monster! You are worse than Seraphina if you keep them locked away like cattle only to let them out so you can gnaw on their necks."

"I do not have other females in this house. And I do not gnaw on anything. I am not an animal," Étienne says through clenched teeth, and I glare at him. "You are my mate. I told you this."

The other two are choking or coughing to cover up the laughter coming out of them in bursts, but new dread spreads through me. They can find humor in my situation all they want, but I will not go quietly from one prison to another. Unlike with Seraphina, I'm going to give these jerks so much hell they'll kick me out of here, prisoner or not.

"Like hell I am."

Looking around, I see a fist-sized crystal ornament under the large vase on the low round table to my right. Snatching it, I cock my hand back and throw it right at his head, but unfortunately, he ducks and it shatters on the wall behind the one with the scar. For some reason, the word mate sounded very romantic the first time he said it, but now something ominous follows when it leaves his mouth. Or I'm scared out of my mind and hurt from them calling me a monster, but I don't care.

"I will not be spreading my legs to have your vampire babies." Reaching for another of the ornaments, I chuck that one too. "Do you even have babies or will bats be ripping through my stomach to get out like in that alien movie? Oh my God! Will I be laying eggs? Its eggs, isn't it? Knowing my luck, it'll be giant ones like an emu or something."

I keep throwing stuff at him, all plans for escaping forgotten at the thought of giant eggs coming out from my

Sound

poor vagina. The other two are now bent over and full on laughing with tears streaming down their faces, but I can't stop what I'm doing. When I run out of smaller things to throw at him, my arms strain when I lift the huge vase. I wobble around and wince from the stinging in my feet—which I completely forgot are even hurt—and I drop it on his legs. He watches me unmoving with an incredulous look on his face. It shatters too, water sloshing over both our feet as flowers fly all over the floor. With my eyes locked on his, I pant like I just ran a marathon, the sound of the vase breaking echoing and bouncing off the walls in the deathly-silent room.

"That vase belonged to our father," Lucien says from somewhere in the room, shock apparent in his tone as if he has just watched me kill a puppy. "Étienne, I don't think she did that on purpose ..."

"I do not care about the fucking vase! Out!" Without looking away from me, he roars, and I jump a foot off the floor at the loud shout.

"Brother ..." The one with the scar lifts off the chair, but Étienne glares at him until he nods once with an apologetic look thrown my way. "You'll be fine, little female." Neither I, nor him, believe those words.

Étienne looks ready to rip me limb from limb.

"I'm not leaving until you calm down," Lucien snaps stubbornly.

"Very well." The sigh coming from me when Étienne answers evenly is short lived.

My shriek makes the other two flinch when I'm lifted over a shoulder, my ass sticking up in the air. My hands grab fistfuls of Étienne's shirt when vertigo makes bile rise in my throat, and my head swivels wildly as I look for something I can grab to hit him with until he puts me down. Nothing is within reach as he strides outside the room with purposeful steps. The last thing I see is Lucien's face, but he isn't scared for me. He isn't even angry. No, he is grinning like he knows something I don't.

That scares me more than anything else in this whole nightmare.

Chapter Twenty-Five

Étienne

I can't decide if I want to kiss her or strangle her. The female is purposely pushing all my buttons to snap the tight control I have on my primal instincts, which are screaming at me to make her fully mine. Having Melody's body so close to me with her scent of blooming roses mingling with that unique one that is all her fills my nostrils and clouds my mind.

My feet beat a harsh rhythm on the wooden floors as I carry her to my rooms where I will keep her until she sees reason—a reason that will not take her away from me. All my well-thought plans go out the window the moment my eyes land on her, and I never think twice whether forging the bond between us is happening too soon. Or if she needed more time to come to terms with it. If she leaves me now ...

I refuse to think of the consequences.

"Put me down you big oaf!" Her small fists thump on

my back and kidneys while I flinch my hips left and right to avoid her kicking feet going straight for my groin. "I'm going to bite you if you don't put me down." She hisses because she's enraged, though I admit my cock stiffens at the idea of her flat teeth on my skin.

I can't hide my groan.

Melody stiffens in my arms.

"Nope!" The last letter makes her lips pop, and I feel the sound through my whole body. "No biting. There will be no biting, you crazy idiot. Who gets turned on by biting, huh?" More punches land on my back. "Vampires, that's who Melody, you dumbass," my mate mutters angrily to herself, not slowing down her attempt to use me as a punching bag. "Just so we are clear, there will be no biting. Now put me down. Right now!"

My hand lands on her round ass—which is way too close to my face and making it impossible not to smell her—with a resounding slap. Her excitement blooms even when she turns as stiff as a board, and I stumble at the top of the stairs, my fangs finally punching out of my gums with a vengeance.

The female will be the death of me, no music needed.

"Did you just spank me?" Shock, embarrassment, and rage are pitching her voice high, and I can't wipe the smirk off my face fast enough. Melody lifts her upper body as high as she can and sees it.

All hell breaks loose.

My mate turns into a wild, angry cat, her tiny hands curled into claws as she swipes her blunt short nails at me anywhere she can reach. Her body turns boneless and she almost slips from my grip when she wiggles violently, bringing her into my arms instead of over my shoulder. Her beautiful doll-like face is bright red, but the glare she gives me will make any human male run as fast as he can. Too bad for my mate I'm neither human nor a coward. Reaching my rooms, I shoulder my way inside, closing the door with a kick of my foot before I drop her on my bed. She grunts once and scurries up the mattress all the way to the headboard while I stand watching her.

"Being a mate doesn't make you a broodmare." Folding my arms across my chest, I stare at her evenly until she stops trying to mold with the headboard.

"Oh yeah? Then what does it make me, huh?"

"Mine!" I have no doubt my brothers hear me all the way down in the living room when I roar in her face. "It makes you mine."

"So you won't make me lay eggs and have bat babies?" Her eyebrows are all the way to her hairline and I can see that she truly believes the nonsense she is saying.

I laugh.

Until a pillow sails through the air and hits me in the head.

"Don't laugh, you jerk. I'm not laying eggs!" Another pillow follows, this one bouncing right off my face. "And I'm not an object. I don't belong to anyone but myself."

"Ah, you see, that's where you are wrong, ma petite." Her frown only makes my smile grow. "Vampires don't lay eggs because we are not chickens." If looks could kill, I would be ashes at the moment. "But don't ever fool yourself into believing that you are not mine. You were born for me, and I will destroy this world if anyone tries to take you away. Do you understand me?"

She stubbornly clams her full mouth shut, shooting daggers at me with her scowl. After I assure myself that she will not move, I step away from the bed, striding to the liquor bar I thankfully have in my rooms. With the conversation I'm about to have with my mate, I'll need a hell of a lot more than a bottle of vino. Snatching a glass, I pour myself three fingers of straight scotch and down it like a shot before refilling the glass. Turning back to face her, I lean back on the bar only to see my mate eyeing me warily.

"That's not blood." She points at the scotch unnecessarily.

"It's scotch." Lifting the glass in a salute, I take a sip of it and let the alcohol burn down my throat while I try to gain a little control so I don't ravish her like a beast. "Would you like some, mon amour?" I realize my mistake when her face blanches. The magic user was forcing her to drink so she could drug her and keep her compliant. "You can have my glass if you wish."

"No, thank you." It kills me to see doubt in her eyes, to know she doesn't trust me. How did things go so wrong?

Fucking Lucien. I should've brought her here first before dealing with my brothers. As much as they mingle with humans, you'd think they'd have more tact. My fingers rub at my forehead while I try to choose the right words to explain things to her. The problem is, I have no idea where to start. I needn't have worried because she decides for me.

"Am I a prisoner?" The sun burning my skin not long ago didn't hurt as much as her question.

"No! Never, Melody." Pushing off the bar, I start to move toward her, but she stiffens and I plop my ass back on it. "Being a mate is not you being a prisoner. Remember the bond I told you about before I marked you?" It takes a long time before she nods, and when she does it's barely a tip of her head. "I cannot forge a bond with just anyone like that. Not unless they were meant for me. We only have one mate, and most of us never find the second part of our soul."

"You are talking about soulmates?" I must've said something right because her shoulders relax, and she leans forward as if eager to hear my answer. "Like when you meet someone and you just click as if you've known them your whole life? That's a mate?"

"In a way ... I suppose that can be a part of it, yes." Judging her reaction over the rim of my glass, I take a longer sip to bide my time. "However, for my kind it's little more than that."

"Like?" Eyes narrowed, my mate watches me like a hawk.

"Now that I have found you and tasted your sweet blood, there will be no other for me." She shivers at my words, and it takes everything in me not to pounce on her. "Not for as long as I'm alive."

"No divorce for vampires, huh?" Her attempt at a light-hearted joke is ruined by the thick swallow that follows.

"Not when we find our mate, no." I still answer regardless of her humor.

"Is this because of what Seraphina said, that I'm a descendant of a god?"

"It could be." Knowing it will be some time before I can get close to her and touch her again, I cross one ankle over the other to get more comfortable for the long conversation ahead. "We are born, not made, and we are long lived. It would be a cruel punishment from the fates to give us a human mate. You being a demigod actually explains how we can be mates. But not why. You are my mate because you are perfect for me."

"You are my mate, too?" Tilting her head to the side, she curls her legs under her, getting more comfortable as well. My heart swells seeing her like that on my bed.

"Can you imagine another male touching you? Kissing your sweet lips? Filling your body with his own?" With each question, I hear her heartbeat speed up, the scent of her arousal saturating the air in the room. "Tell me, Melody. Can you allow another male to sink his cock inside you and fill you up?" Despite all the tells she involuntarily offers through the reaction of her body, I hold my breath waiting for her answer.

I should've known better.

My mate is a feisty little thing, and she will make me work for every little thing she gives me. The bar cracks under my tight grip when she smiles sweetly at me and speaks the worst thing you can say to a male like me.

"And what if I can? What are you going to do about it?"

The hard thump of my heart against the breastbone curls the corners of my lips up and the smile grows when I watch her shiver when she sees it.

Chapter Twenty-Six

Melody

I don't know why, but the need to piss him off is stronger than my will to keep breathing, at least if I judge by the way the wood cracks when Étienne's hand tightens around it. My heart somersaults at the smirk and the feral look in his blue eyes, but deep down some alien part of me rejoices at the reaction. With bated breaths, I watch him lower the glass gently on the bar, but when he swaggers toward me, I jump off the bed with a scream.

My feet tangle on the soft bed covers and I tumble off the tall mattress, ending up in a heap on the floor. The pain I should be feeling is a distant tingling through my limbs because the white noise in my ears from the blood rushing through my veins is much louder. Another scream escapes me when two strong arms pluck me off the ground, and I find myself face to face with Étienne.

"Why do you wish to anger me, little one?" His blue eyes flash for a second, and that wreaks havoc on my body.

"Your lips say one thing"—His thumb glides over my lower lip, pulling gently down on it—"but your body tells me something else."

"What, you are a body language expert now?" My voice sounds breathless, and I want to slap him when he grins knowingly at me.

"I can smell you, little Muse." Étienne outright laughs at the horrified look that's spreading over my face. "I can feel your desire dampening your panties when I'm near you. Tell me, Melody, how wet are they right now, love?" he whispers in my ear before pulling away just enough to see my bright red face.

Lips dry and tongue sticking to the roof of my mouth, I can't answer him or tell him to go to hell, not even if it will save my life. Held captive in his intense blue gaze, I stand frozen while his hands roam all over my body, not really touching but close enough I can feel the heat of his skin burning me through the clothing. My nerve endings are tingling everywhere his hands pass, and it feels like he is branding me all over without placing a finger on me. That changes really fast, too. Fast enough I have no time to react before he murmurs again, his deep voice rumbling in his chest.

"I can hear the speeding of your heartbeat the second you sense me near you." One graceful finger glides from the hollow of my neck down between my breasts, stopping just above my treacherous heart. "It beats in sync with mine. Do you know why that is, little Muse?" Like a dumbass, all I can do is shake my head no. "Because this right here, Melody …" His finger thumps gently on my ribs. "This is mine."

"Arrogant much, Ethan?" My attempt at a bravado and the butchering of his name goes down the drain when his grin grows like the cat that ate the canary.

"Shall we see if it is arrogance or simply the truth?"

He doesn't allow me to argue, killing my rebuttal by grabbing the shirt I'm wearing on each side, and with one harsh tug he rips it off me. One strong arm wraps around my waist, and he yanks me to his chest crushing his mouth on mine. Every rational thought leaves my mind and my fingers tangle in his shirt as I pull him closer so he can't escape. The butterflies are having a rave party in my belly, and I press closer to him like feeling his hard body molding to my soft one is not enough. When his tongue dives between my lips and entwines with mine, soft groans and moans are ripped from me that only urge him on.

The next thing to turn to shreds are my pants, leaving me trembling in his arms in my panties. The chilled air brushes across my skin when the room spins and my back hits the soft mattress. I blink up at Etienne, who is looming over me still fully dressed. Embarrassed, I twist around to hide my nakedness from his hungry gaze, but he won't have any of it. With one hand firmly pressed on my hip, he holds me in place, his blue eyes roaming over me as if he is devouring every bit of bare skin he can see.

"Magnifique. You are magnificent, mon amour." Lowering his head, he presses his lips softly on mine before locking gazes with me. "Don't hide from me, little one. I have not seen anything more beautiful or more perfect for me in all my long years."

There is no doubt in my mind that he is telling the truth. The sincerity is written clearly in the blue depths of his eyes, so I stop struggling to hide myself from him. At this very moment I can't understand why I wanted to run from him. The overwhelming need to run and hide from this fantastical world I find myself in disappears like it never existed, and I lose myself in the safety Étienne's arms provide. Clarity that there is no escape from this crashes into me, and with it comes the only thing I need to know. My life might've turned inside out with magic, vampires, witches, and whatnot, but with him by my side, I feel that I can find my place in it all. I don't have to hide anymore. I'm no longer a freak who kills people with her music. Being surrounded by his body over me should be intimidating. It should scare me, but it feels safe. Not like a cage to keep me in, but like a shield to keep everything and everyone out. A peculiar realization to have while sprawled naked under the most beautiful man I've ever seen, but there it is.

"Thank you." Tears prickle my eyes when I whisper my gratitude.

"Whatever for, little one?" A line forms between his eyebrows as he peers down at me, his blond hair tousled from my fingers running through it earlier when he was kissing me.

"For hearing me in the silence?" My voice thick with emotion, I let him see everything I feel, everything that is choking me at the moment. "For staying after the music stopped? For saving me? You name it." A sob-laugh escapes me before I can stop it. "For dealing with my tantrum earlier? I didn't act very grateful and I'm sorry. Sorry for hitting you, as well," I add lamely.

"You have nothing to apologize for, Melody." He moves strands of hair away from my face, his eyes mapping every blink of my lashes, every breath passing my lips. "After everything you've been through, little one, I must say I'm impressed that you held on so well for that long. You have every right to break down." I frown at him, and he softens his tone. "Do you know why?"

"Why?"

"Because no matter how many times you break, I'll

always be here to help put you back together. So break away, my little Muse, because I'll be right where I am when you come back from it." The small smile playing on his lips is fascinating. No one has ever looked at me with that much tenderness.

"Thank you." My trembling hand finds his face and he nuzzles my palm. "I don't know why I started acting the way I did. It's like something possessed me and all I wanted to do was make you angry." Admitting my weakness is not easy, but I push the words out.

"Ah, but I know." Tugging the shirt over his head, he presses me into the mattress and my breath hitches when I feel him skin on skin. "Your bloodline was awakened, and you are not trying to make me angry, little one. You are challenging me to see if I'm a worthy mate."

"I don't know what that means." I gasp when his lips start moving across my neck and collar bone.

"I'm about to show you." Goosebumps pop up all over my arms and legs when he whispers in my ear.

Chapter Twenty-Seven

Étienne

Her skin is like silk under my hands, and every sound she makes is driving me insane. Not even the tracks left from the tears she has shed can take away from her beautiful doll-like face. The dark curls spread around her head like a cloud, and I'm humbled the gates saw me worthy of such a beauty. If I didn't know she was of the lineage of the Muses, I would think Aphrodite herself has offered me one of her daughters.

"Étienne ..." My mate moans impatiently, but I cannot stop touching her.

"What is it, little Muse. Tell me what you need." The groan rumbling my chest can't be stopped when my tongue glides across her skin, her taste filling all my senses.

"I ... Oh my God ... I need ... I have no idea what I need." Her back arches while her little fingers claw at my shoulders, and it takes everything in me not to sink my throbbing fangs in her neck.

Sound

"I might have a clue what you need, love."

Ducking my head, I take her breast in my hand and twirl my tongue around a pebbled nipple. Melody moans a low, raspy sound that makes me so hard the zipper of my pants is painfully pressed against my cock. Releasing the tight peak with a pop, I kiss my way down her body, swirling my tongue around her bellybutton and moving lower still without giving her time to realize what I'm planning. Melody jerks up, lifting on her elbows to stare at me wide-eyed, her lips parted in shock when I push my way between her thighs, throwing each of her legs over a shoulder.

"Umm, what are—oh!" she exclaims when I dive between her folds, her arousal drenching my mouth. "Oh my God!"

Holding her captive with my gaze, I lick and suck on her button, pushing my tongue inside her tight channel. I want to roar in pride when her eyes roll and she takes the covers in her fists. Melody's sweetness floods my senses, and I take my time pleasuring my mate until her body stiffens and the mewls coming from her lips turn loud and protesting. Still, I continue eating her up, her juices tasting better than any blood ever has.

"Étienne!" She explodes screaming my name and I swallow everything her body gives like a male dying from thirst. Leisurely my tongue swirls around her button and across her folds until she is a twitching and quivering mess under my lips.

"I think I just died," Melody gasps, her voice sounding raw from the screaming.

"Not yet, love." Her half-lidded eyes widen when I lift from between her thighs and lick her juices off my lips. "We are nowhere near done here."

She tracks my fingers, not even blinking as I pull the

zipper of my pants down in a tantalizing move. The rasp of the metal fills the room and her skin pebbles. Dropping the offending fabric around my ankles, I kick off my shoes, too, leaving me, standing naked above her. Her eyes are glued to my bobbing erection like she's never seen anything like it, and I pause wondering if my mate has ever been with a male before. I never stopped to think about it, but now looking at my length and girth, doubt creeps in and freezes my movements. I'll have to take it slow and get her accustomed to me.

Then she licks her lips, her thighs shifting restlessly on the covers, and all my well meanings and control go out the window.

Covering her body with mine, electricity buzzes under my skin everywhere our bodies are connected. Taking hold of her hands, I lace our fingers together and push her arms above her head, crushing my mouth on hers. My mate gives as good as she gates, her tongue sparring with mine in a primal dance of all ages. I feel her powers coming to the surface, tentatively first but soon like a current merging with mine.

Melody opens her legs wider to nestle me between her thighs, and I groan when my cock slides up and down her wet folds every time she arches her back or tries to get closer. Swallowing her moans, I rock my hips into her, and she responds immediately, perfectly matching my movements. Unable to hold back any longer, I take both her wrists in one hand while running the other from her neck down to her hip where I press her into the mattress so she can't move. Even in the feral state she has brought me to, I still don't want to hurt her.

"Hold still, love." The words are rasped through my fangs, and the urgency I see on her face claws at my insides.

Sound

Guiding the tip of my cock to her entrance, I nudge her gently, allowing the head to enter her channel without pressing too hard. Her tight walls clench around me and suck me in until I have to grind my teeth so I don't bury myself all the way to the hilt in one hard thrust. Rocking in and out, with each push forward I sink deeper, her hot opening stretching and giving way to accommodate me. It's pure torture to hold back, but I have to do it for her. If I hurt her in any way, I'll never forgive myself. And just then the vixen moves, her hips jerking hard off the bed to shove me all the way in, my balls slapping the round globes of her ass.

My groan is drowned by her loud moans.

"Étienne." Melody gasps and wiggles her hips. "Étienne …"

"Easy love, I don't want to hurt you."

"If you don't fuck me and start moving, I will hurt you," my mate growls, glaring at me while I hold still above her as stiff as a board.

"Who am I to deny you, little Muse." With a feral grin that hitches her breath, I release her wrists and take hold of her hips with both hands.

Pulling back as far as I can go to just have the tip of my cock inside her, I stand still for just a second before thrusting hard and rocking her body up the bed. Melody screams as her tiny fingers wrap around my forearms so I don't push her too far away. My hips start pistoning between her thighs, the slapping of flesh against flesh filling up the vast room. Her channel milks my hard cock every time I pull back, sucking me back in while her juices run down her thighs and soak us both.

I lose myself inside my mate, our powers merging just as our bodies are connected as one. Melody's head turns left and right, her chin lifted in bliss and her eyes closed. I've never seen a more beautiful sight than my mate in the throes of passion. It feeds my own pleasure until the bond we partly forged when I bit her blooms to life, calling me to complete it in the most primal of ways. I still hold back, unsure of how she will react if I bare my fangs at her while she's vulnerable underneath me like this. My mate surprises me yet again, her instincts that woke up with her bloodline leading her actions.

Melody bares her neck.

The movement is so submissive, yet her body language is more dominant than any I've ever seen. Her hands tug on my forearms and urge me to lower myself, while her back lifts off the bed to bring her closer.

With a growl ripped from the center of my chest, I sink my fangs in her long, graceful neck just as my cock sinks inside her to the hilt. My balls are tingling when her blood floods my mouth, and I gulp it down greedily. The orgasm catches Melody first, and her walls tighten around me so hard I find it difficult to move. My name screamed from between her lips triggers my own peak, and jerking my head up, I roar her name to the heavens while pulsing violently inside her, my seed flooding her insides. Our bodies keep rocking in sync as power swirls around us, some distant luring music filling my ears and entering my pores through every gasped breath I take. Melody's voice echoes along with mine until both of us are raw.

Rolling to the side, I pull her along with me until her body is draped over mine, though my cock is still hard inside her. She doesn't protest, but tiny gasps of air pass her lips and puff across my chest when she pillows her face on it. Wrapping my arms around her, I hold her as tight as I can without crushing her, silently vowing that I will kill anyone that dares even think to take her from me.

"Holy shit. What was that?" Melody rasps, raising her head to peer at me through her lashes. "I swear my soul just left my body." She bursts into giggles and I can't help but smile at her.

"It was the bond forming as it was completed that made it so intense." Moving the strands of hair sticking to the sides of her sweaty face, I watch her carefully. "Did I hurt you?"

"If that's your idea of hurting, you can hurt me like that anytime you want." More giggles follow, and she ducks her head to hide the reddening of her cheeks. "I swear I'm possessed. I don't usually say everything that's on my mind."

"I want to know everything that's on your mind, love." Bringing her face up again with a finger under her chin, I smile at her embarrassment. "I love seeing you like this." My thumb glides across her warm cheek. "It suits you, little Muse."

"What suits me?" She blinks at me in confusion.

"Being well pleasured, with your hair wild from my fingers and your lips swollen from my kisses."

"It must be that whole European thing helping, since you know all the right things to say to make a girl swoon, Étienne." She slaps me playfully on the chest and I laugh. "Let me go, I need to dress."

"I don't think so, love." She opens her glistening lips to protest, but I'm already moving in and out of her, making her moan instead of speak. I'm not done with you yet. Nowhere near done."

My mate's screams and moans echo for many more hours through the night. It's the best music my little Muse could play for me.

Chapter Twenty-Eight

Melody

I watch Étienne's face as he sleeps next to me, though internally I'm fighting the panic trying to bubble up because I had sex with a vampire and when he bit me something inside me changed fundamentally. His long, thick lashes cast shadows over his high cheekbones, and his kissable lips are slightly parted. Sleep softens his normally controlled features making him so adorable my fingers twitch with the need to touch him. Unable to stop myself, I gently move the few strands of blond hair that fall over his forehead and freeze when his deep, even breathing changes.

Holding my own breath, I wait to see if his eyes will open, but he stays in whatever dreamland he is in right now. The urge to giggle like an idiot is there, and the stupid smile on my face hurts my cheeks. I never knew sex could be so intense or life altering. Everything he said about mates and how I am it for him better be true, because after the night we had I have not an ounce of doubt that he broke me for

Sound

any other man. I wasn't even sure my body was capable of so many orgasms in one night.

Delicious soreness left as a reminder of what happened between us tingles on the inside of my thighs, so I shift my legs and pull the covers down, revealing Étienne's bare shoulders and chest. My eyes roam across every dip and bulge of his muscles, and then his right arm—which is curled around me protectively—tightens to pull me closer to him. Even in his sleep he keeps me close so he can protect me from anything trying to harm me.

The room is dark since the thick heavy drapes are closed over the windows, though a soft light from the handful of tall lamps casts a golden glow on his skin. All the furniture is made of solid, polished wood, carved expertly to look like art pieces rather than something one would use in a bedroom. Earthy tones give it a comforting feel, from the crème colored walls to the light brown upholstery on the ornate chair, which is placed next to a round little table with leather bound tomes of old books that form a small tower on it. Even the candelabra, with one long white candle stuck in it and the wax hardened along its tall body, makes me feel like I've stepped into a different time and space.

The second I stepped foot inside his home, I was left gaping at all the opulent things arranged tastefully in every hallway and room. From golden accents on the walls, to the statues and sculptures perched on their own stands, to the paintings sprinkled between them that belong more to a museum than a house, I was left dumbfounded feeling like I stepped through history into some eighteenth century royal court. After the events that transpired at the cursed place where Seraphina held me prisoner, me and my bloody feet, along with my dirty clothes and smudged face, don't belong here.

I don't belong here.

Étienne's arm tugs me closer to his chest and the feel of his skin on mine makes me sigh deeply, all the air exiting my lungs in one long exhale. If I don't belong here, than why does it feel so right? Why do I have this sense of rightness deep in my soul, this awareness that in his arms is where I was meant to be all along? While his handsome face nuzzles the crook of my neck, my mind wanders off back to everything I learned about myself.

A descendant of a god.

Me.

The girl that barely had any friends, who clutched her violin like a shield against the world until Viola decided to befriend me and refused to go away and leave me alone. The freak everyone used to whisper about in the hallways of the school whenever I passed by.

A demigod.

Unhinged laughter tries to bubble out of me, but I swallow it down because I don't want to wake Étienne. Goosebumps pebble my skin just thinking of what could've happened if I didn't go with Viola to keep her company when she wanted to see her sister. If I hadn't been in the club that evening when Étienne came out of nowhere and made me think I was hallucinating when he spoke. I've never given fate or destinies much thought, but looking back at events now, everything seems to have been orchestrated to bring me here. I don't even want to think about what could've happened if he never saw me that night. If he didn't know I existed, would he still have done everything he had to save me when Salmon lured him to the Chalice? Guilt rears its head when I realize I keep calling Alto Salmon like he is just a cat. He is not a cat ... far from it actually.

Sound

And you are not human either.

Chills spread through my body, numbing me from head to toe when a voice inside my head reminds me of that. Lost in my thoughts, I don't hear Étienne wake until he speaks, and I have to bite on my lip so I don't scream when he breaks the silence.

"What has you thinking so hard, little Muse? I can hear the gears turning in that brain of yours in my sleep." His deep voice is raspy from sleep, and it does all sorts of inappropriate things to my insides. I'm taken aback all over again when I turn to look at him and his lashes flutter before he lazily opens his eyes. I lose myself in the deep blue of his irises. A small smile tilts his lips at my reaction. "I thought I tired you enough to stop fretting, though it would seem I was wrong yet again when it comes to you, little mate."

"Hey," is all I can whisper because butterflies are flapping through my stomach due to the way he is looking at me.

"Hey," Étienne whispers back like his word is some great secret we are sharing. "What has you awake, Melody, when you should be resting? I thought being well pleasured and cleaned up would have you sleeping for days." That's when I realize my hair is soft and clean, and so is my body. He must've washed me when I passed out in his arms. Becoming more alert, he lifts himself on one elbow and peers down at me anxiously. "Are you hungry? I never stopped to think that you need food."

As if summoned, my stomach growls so loud it sounds like a hungry bear ready to attack its pray. My face catches on fire from embarrassment. The thought of food didn't even register until he mentioned it. When his body coils to move, I take hold of the arm he still has around me to keep him next to me.

"Do you think I have some powers now? Apart from my music killing people, do I have other powers after as you say my bloodline woke up?" It's strange that my fingers are cold while his skin is so warm at the touch.

"What do you need powers for, little Muse?" A line forms between his eyebrows and I smooth it with my thumb.

"You promised that you'd save my friends from Seraphina, remember?" Holding my breath, my hand tightens on him while I wait for his answer. I hope he hasn't changed his mind because I pissed him off so much with my little tantrum last night.

"I always keep my word, love." Placing a soft kiss on my lips, he moves away so he can look into my eyes. "We will get them out of there and kill the magic user that hurt you. I swear it on my life."

"I want to help." I know the second I speak that I'm going to have to fight him to be involved in the rescue, but I'm nothing if not stubborn. It's what kept me alive the whole time I was held captive. "I am going to help, Étienne, whether you like it or not. They are my friends, and it's partly my fault they are in this mess. If I didn't agree to go to that audition, neither Viola nor Harmony would've been there in the first place."

"You are not going anywhere near that place, Melody. And that's final." Throwing the covers off him, he jumps out of bed angrily but I'm finding it hard to remember what we were talking about when his naked body rises next to the bed. "My brothers and I will deal with the witch and save your friends from that cursed place." Whirling around, whatever he was going to add in his anger trails off and he smirks at my gaping face. "You like what you see, little mate? I can stay naked forever if that will keep you from arguing."

"I'm drooling, aren't I?" I stupidly murmur and even wipe my mouth with the back of my hand to check. Yup, drooling. His grin grows, and I shake my head to clear it, dragging my eyes away from his nakedness and back to his handsome face. "No. Don't you fucking distract me! I'm going. I can stay in the background while the three of you do your thing," I rush to assure him, but those assurances are only good if he agrees to take me along. "You won't even know I'm there. Scout's honor."

"Fat chance that I won't know you are there, love." His gaze turns hungry as he looks me up and down, and that's when I notice when he stood, the covers slipped. Now they are pooling around my waist, so I snatch them and tuck them under my while I glare at him.

"They won't come with you if I'm not there, Étienne." Changing tactics, I try for reason. "They've been prisoners just like me. Do you think they'll follow strange men after what they've been through?"

"You did."

I hate that he is right.

"But I'd already seen you and spoken to you once before. They haven't." Seeing his determination wavering, I push my advance, lifting on my knees and clutching the covers like a safety blanket. "I promise I'll listen to everything you say. I won't twitch a finger unless you tell me to. Please."

Heart hammering in my chest and lungs burning from holding my breath, I watch his lips part and wait for his decision. My body lifts a foot off the bed, and I shriek like an idiot when a fist thumps in rapid fire on the door.

"Can you two have this conversation downstairs?" Lucien grumbles from behind the closed door. "We can hear every word, anyway. At least we won't feel like creeps if we can see you."

"Oh my God!" I whisper breathlessly, staring wide-eyed at Étienne. "They heard everything …"

I toss a pillow at his face when he throws his head back and laughs.

Chapter Twenty-Nine

Étienne

My mind is still reeling from Melody's arguments to join us to rescue her friends. Keeping an eye on her as she sways her hips in front of me down the hallway, I fight my own logic to find one good reason to keep her hidden here in the house until the magic user and everyone she works with are dead. It sounds like a solid plan in theory, but the fact that she will be alone while I'm across town doesn't sit well with me. Her hair moves across her back as she looks around at everything like a child in a candy shop, her brown eyes alight in wonder. Warmth spreads through my chest because she seems to like what we have done with our home.

All contentment leaves my body the moment we enter my office and find the solemn faces of my brothers watching us. Melody stops in her tracks as if unsure whether she should enter or bolt back to hide in my rooms. I can see from her body language that she wants to run. Not giving her time to do that, I place a hand at the small of her back and guide her inside, closing the door behind me just in case she changes her mind. Moving my reluctant mate through the office and around my desk, I wait until she gingerly lowers in my chair, and only then do I step behind it to lean on the backrest behind her.

"Hello again, Melody." Moël breaks the silence, his features all apologetic as he addresses my mate. "We didn't have a good start and it was my fault. I didn't mean to sound like I didn't want you here, or to imply that you will turn against my brother." With a sigh, he shakes his head, but it's more to himself than anyone else. "I'm not used to having others around when discussing things with my brothers. I was simply stating facts that I have learned."

"You don't have to say sorry to me." Melody's voice is hesitant at first, but each word she speaks gets stronger until the woman I met the first time I saw her comes to the surface. "You didn't make up crap just to say bad things about me, I'm sure. The fact is that neither the three of you nor I know anything about what I am and what I can do … apart from killing people when I play, that is. I'd be wary, too, if I were you. Is Salmon…" her voice trails off before she grimaces shaking her head. "Is Alto okay? The cat."

"He is well, yes." Moël assures her. "After Lucien healed him we left him to rest and recover in my room. He is much safer there than around any of us at the moment."

My mouth opens to tell her that she has nothing to worry about, but she cuts of my words before they even form on my tongue.

"Thank you, both of you." There is no mistaking the sincerity in her voice. "What I can promise you is that I have no intention of hurting any of you. As I said, I'll never play the violin again. Not if I can help it." My heart breaks at the sadness she is trying to hide.

Sound

"I don't think that's an option, little demigod," Lucien grumbles where he is leaning on the wall with his arms crossed across his chest.

"I swear the next person who calls me 'little' will have that violin broken over their head, and then I'll have nothing to play even if I want to." she snaps at both of them, and my lips quirk when my brothers gawk at my mate. "I'm not *little*, and it's not my fault the three of you are huge, okay? We don't make people that big in America, not unless they play basketball. So stop being an ass. And if I don't want to play, no one can make me. Not unless they do it against my will like Seraphina did. But I'll never let that happen again if I can help it, so that is not an option."

"I like her." Moël grins at me over her head, while Melody and Lucien glare at each other.

"The blood of a Muse runs through your veins," Lucien snarls at her, his upper lip curling above his fangs until his eyes flick my way. At my scowl, he schools his features and speaks to my mate with more respect. "Tell me, when you didn't play your precious violin, did you feel like yourself? Or did it feel like a limb was missing and you moved through life like a tumbleweed drifting in the breeze?"

"How could you possibly know that?" Melody whispers, her face blanched and hands fisted in her lap. My body stiffens like a rock hearing Lucien's words.

"It doesn't take a genius to know this." Shifting uncomfortably when we all stare at him, my middle brother shrugs as if trying for nonchalance. "Just like we are if we don't take blood." This is said while he looks at me pointedly, reminding me of our regular argument about me not feeding. "So would you be, if you didn't play music. You are a descendant of the Muse of music, so it makes sense that you will need the sound to function properly."

"Are you saying I have to kill people to feel normal? To stay alive?" Jumping off the chair, Melody turns her frightened gaze my way. "I can never live with myself if I have to do that, Étienne. Just kill me and get it over with, please."

"No one is killing anyone." Taking her hand, I tug her under my arm. My chest swells when she comes willingly, molding to me like she belongs there. "When I heard your music, every time it only lured me to you. It was like a call I couldn't resist, but apart from that it did no harm." A white lie since I almost walked into the daylight many times while hearing it in my dreams. I would walk in the daylight now without the music calling me for her. "It's with good reason to believe we can hear you play the violin without any harm coming to us at all."

"I wish I could kill Seraphina with it. That death wouldn't make me lose sleep at all," my fierce mate mumbles, and I can't help but chuckle at that. "What are we going to do now?" Peeking at me from beneath her lashes, she blushes when my hungry gaze devours her beautiful face, my skin buzzing through the clothing where I feel her softness pressing against me. "When are we going after Vi and Harmony?"

"Are they descendants from the same Muse?" Moël's question is as if someone pressed pause in the room.

I never even thought of that. Are my mate's friends the same as her. Going on a hunch from what little we remembered of my father's words, all of us assumed that all three females were the same. We are brothers, after all, and regardless of our different personalities and our unique trades, we are very much alike in many ways other than our uncanny resemblance. With that another thought comes uninvited, and my eyes lock first on Moël's, and then on Lucien's. How are we going to find the other two females if we don't hear them play? Racking my brain, my blood chills in my veins when I remember that last night after I finally allowed my mate to sleep. I didn't hear any music.

Not even a note.

"What is it?" Melody steps away from me, her concern-filled eyes never leaving mine. "What's going on Étienne?"

"I heard nothing," Moël says under his breath before scratching at the scar on his face, and Melody's head whips in his direction.

"Same here," Lucien mutters with a scowl that twists his features.

"What does that mean?" Tugging on my arm, she gets louder. "What didn't you hear?"

"Music." Speaking slowly, I glance between my brothers. "We found you, and I was there just in time because we heard your music. It appears that we can't hear it anymore."

"And?" My mate is getting frantic, and fear is written all over her porcelain face. I pull her into my arms.

"We will find a way, little Muse. I promise, we'll find them." A grunt bursts from my lips when her little fist wedges itself in my gut.

"Stop calling me little," she hisses against my chest, and Moël barks out a laugh, covering it with a cough when I glare at him. Even Lucien is fighting a grin, the grumpy bastard. "I know!" Melody's voice is muffled from my shirt, so she shoves with both hands for me to release her. I reluctantly do, much to my brothers' amusement.

"What is that, love? What do you know?" Rubbing at my stomach where she practiced her obviously good right hook, I look down at her.

"There is this song." Lucien groans at that, but my shark-like look cuts off his bullshit. Melody glares at him for a long moment too before slowly turning back to face me. "As I was saying before I was rudely interrupted"—Moël chuckles and her lips twitch for a second, but she continues enthusiastically—"there is this song that we played ever since we became friends. We kinda made it up, but anyway ... I know for sure that if she hears me play the first notes, Viola will follow along. If I'm close enough to where she can hear me, I have no doubt I'll hear her as well."

"It sounds like a good plan to me," Moël pipes in, and Melody smiles at him so sweetly I want to punch his smug face. "It's the only one we have, but it's good, nonetheless. I'm game."

"I see you found a way to make sure that you are not left behind, little Muse." Shaking my head, I chuckle when her fists flies at my face, but I snatch her hand in my palm and tug her back into my arms. "Let us try it your way."

"We will be there, brother." All humor forgotten, Moël regards me evenly. "We won't allow anything to happen to your mate."

"Thank you, brother. I will hold you to your word." Arm tightening around Melody, I can't help the trepidation coursing through my veins.

"Very well. Let's go get the damn females out. I need to kill something; it's been too long," Lucien growls with a feral look in his eyes, and Melody shrinks into me.

"You can stop being an asshole now, Lucien. After all, one of the said females could be your mate," Moël snaps, and much to my pleasure, Lucien's face drains of all the color.

" Que le destin nous vienne en aide." My middle brother sounds like he is about to faint, and both Moël and I burst out laughing.

Sound

"What did he say?" Melody pokes me in the ribs to get my attention and I wink down at her.

"He said fates help us, but I think what he meant to say was, he is fucked."

We all laugh, the joyful sound echoing through the room while Lucien looks like he would like nothing more than to rip our hands off.

"Oh, that's a given. If either Viola or Harmony are his mate, I can guarantee that he is fucked." Melody giggles, gleefully staring at Lucien. A payback for being an ass in front of her this whole time, I'm sure.

Nothing could wipe the smug grin off my face.

Next in The Last Note Series

vinci-books.com/sonata

Freedom comes with a price. Is her heart the cost?

Viola's violin was her escape—until it lured an evil witch who imprisoned her and her friends. Just when hope seemed lost, a stranger shattered the curse. She should be celebrating her freedom, but now she faces a new danger: will he break more than just the spell?

Turn the page for a free preview…

Sonata: Chapter One

Viola

Music is life.

Or death.

It really depends on which way you look at it. For me personally, it proved not so positive a while back at a concert when two of my best friends and I had dreams of being famous, making a ton of money, and touring the world doing what we loved. Dozens of people died, leaving all of us broken in more ways than we knew at the time. It not only screwed with our music, but it shattered something in our souls, too. Subconsciously, I rubbed a hand at the center of my chest before catching myself and tightly fisting my hand. I refused to think of those days; it won't do me any good between the four walls closing me on all sides.

That same ambition which the other two ladies dropped like a hot potato, made me drag them to this cursed place and got all of us imprisoned by a creature of nightmares. Oh, she looked very much angelic, and lovely, and normal...human. But every other day, as I watched either of my friends play their instruments while their audience withered and turned to husks in front of my eyes, it only cemented my conviction. She was something other, and the talent for music for all three of us was not life but death...

And I was the furthest thing from a human, too.

People didn't just do the things the three of us were capable of. It wasn't just my friends taking lives with their music. It was me too. I did that. The fact I was forced because not me, but my friends will suffer for my refusal did not justify it. It actually sounded like a very lame excuse even to my own ears. Is this why all the musical geniuses of all times went insane? It was a ridiculous thought, I was well aware of that, but you can never know.

I mean, it's not like I expected to be taken by a monster, so the crazy thought might carry weight. These days I simply didn't know what to think or believe. Apart from the fact that my captor was definitely a heinous bitch.

Grinding my teeth, I took long deep breaths to calm my thoughts. Talking crap about another woman only made you feel better because if you convinced yourself she sucks, while you envy her at the same time, it meant she's not as impressive or unique as she appears to be. It's been my mission in life to empower women, and yet here I was, having these damn thoughts poisoning my mind.

"This is not you, Viola. You're better than this." Muttering under my breath, I focused on my breathing.

The musty stench of the damp walls clung to my nostrils, heavy with mold and what I knew now to be magic. My lungs sagged heavily in my chest as if filled with water, and I struggled to keep my inhales even and calm. Aware that my mind had a lot more to do with how I was reacting to my situation than anything else, my eyes opened on the next exhale. It was all a mind game that Seraphina played with us, and if I could only find a weakness in her plans, I was sure that I can get us out of the cursed place.

A church of all places nonetheless.

How's that for a slap in the face?

My breathing sped up, and I darted my gaze around the room or my prison because that's what it was, focusing on physical things to stop the building panic attack. As long as I can see objects that I could touch, it helped ground me in the present and out of the wild thoughts churning in my brain. A couple of days in a row, I thought I heard music coming from the outside too, the melody similar to a song my friends and I made up ages ago teasing my senses. I also played at those times, which kept me from screaming help as loud as I could. No one but the three of us knew that song, so I was aware that it was my imagination since we were all locked in the damn place, but it did make me feel closer to the other two women when the notes filled the small room.

It took me a long moment to hear the soft purring coming from around my cold feet. Without missing a beat, I reached out and pulled the cat to my chest, wrapping my arms around the soft furry body and clinging to it like a lifeline. The purr intensified as I buried my face in the cat and filled my nose with the musky scent of the animal. Someone once told me that cats are susceptible to human emotions, making them perfect companions for those suffering from anxiety and depression. Although I was up to my eyeballs in the wild woman, awaken your inner goddess movement, I never actually got one for myself.

In the middle of my nightmare life, he found me.

It was the only thing protecting my sanity.

"Hey, buddy. You came again." Whispering so he

Sound

doesn't freak out and claws my eyes out, I rubbed my cheek on his fur. "I missed you for a few days."

I'll never admit to a soul that I actually worried about the rascal when he didn't show up each day thinking that crazy woman found him and killed him. Melody, Harmony, and I were still alive because she had a use for us. I was sure of that. The cat, on the other hand? Not so much, from what I could see. He always hid when Seraphina showed up. Not that I blamed him.

A loud mewl came from the small body in my arms, and he stretched lazily, almost falling out of my hold. Scooting back on the small bed where I slept every night, I leaned my back on the wall to give him more room to wiggle. Having him near calmed me down unlike anything else. Sinking my fingers in his soft coat, I scraped my nails gently, which usually made him roll on his back and enjoy the scratches. However, his time he stiffened, and one of his ears flicked this way and that while his eyes were locked on the wall to my left.

There were no windows in this room, and the only way in and out was through the locked wooden door that looked flimsy but not even a truck can break through it. I know because I tried everything the first few days I got locked here. From throwing the one chair that ended up with a cracked leg which will eventually give out while I'm putting mascara on, and I'll poke my eye out. Taking a running start and slamming the metal bed frame at it that resulted in me biting my tongue from the impact might've been smarter, but the door didn't move. I even pulled a ninja on it, jumping and kicking at it, shouting like a banshee for sound effects. It sounded nuts now, but at the time, it was a good idea. I've seen Karate Kid a dozen times, so I thought I can totally pull it off.

Daniel San, I was not.

A girl can dream, but the door stayed locked and I was left a prisoner.

At least I had the cat, and occasionally I saw Melody and Harmony. They were still alive, and so was I. Things could've been much worse. My violin caught my attention from the corner of my eye, propped on the dresser, taunting me. With clenched teeth, I glared at it as if everything was the instrument's fault. I had to blame something or someone for everything, and if it wasn't my violin, then I'll have to admit we were all locked up by a psycho because of me. I wasn't sure I could handle the guilt in my fragile mental state, so I hardened my stare. In my turmoil, I must've cramped my fingers because the cat hissed, sinking its claws in my thigh before jumping off my lap with a screech.

"Crap." Scrambling off the bed, I dropped on my knees on the dirty floor, the hard impact jarring my bones. "I'm so sorry, buddy, so... so... sorry. Please don't leave."

Tears burned at the back of my eyes while I lifted my hand, reaching out palm up, begging him not to disappear. I was so messed up, I scared the only living creature that kept me company because I couldn't control my emotions. The cat eyed me warily, ears pinned to its skull and upper lip curled so he can bare his teeth. The long tail lashed behind him in agitation, but it was his stare that sent a shiver to crawl up my spine. I knew he was an animal, but there was uncanny intelligence meeting my gaze that made my body go cold and numb.

"I'm sorry." I breathed through unmoving lips feeling dazed by the vertical pupils.

That's the only reason I jumped a foot off the floor when a scrape of a shoe came from behind the wall—the brick and mortar barrier to my freedom. The cat smirked,

Sound

which confirmed I was ready for the mental hospital and already had my mind on vacation while I wobbled around on all fours to face whatever insanity was coming from me. Another scrape of a pebble over hard ground formed goosebumps on my arms, sending my heart rate into overdrive while I panted like a crazy woman with wild eyes.

"You are imagining things Viola, get a grip." It didn't sound as firm as I wanted when my voice cracked, but beggars can't be choosers and all that. "Snap out of it woman, you are your worst enemy. You are hearing things."

I knew it was my mind playing tricks on me because apart from the car and Seraphina, no other sound has ever reached my ears in this room. Be it as it may, my heart was still galloping against my ribs, and my breaths were coming in short, harsh puffs. It all stopped, my heart, my breathing, even my mind went blank when a distant voice started spitting words I couldn't understand, but I could've bet my life they were coming from a person standing on the other side of that wall.

An embarrassing scream ripped from my throat when the cat nudged me on my side with his body. Hands shaking and body trembling, I scowled at him, but he only bared his sharp teeth again and swatted at me claws and all. Forgetting all about the voice, I moved as fast as I could so the cat didn't cut me with those dagger-like nails without realizing he was hoarding me toward the dresser. The same dresser with a mirror perched on top of it pressed against the wall where the person was still angrily now growling foreign words.

My hip bumped into the unforgiving corner of the dresser toppling over the bottles and makeup neatly placed on it when I caught up with what the little bugger was doing. Anger bubbled up in my chest, mostly from fear than anything else, and I pushed myself up on my feet, snatching the violin as I went. Grinding my teeth, I swung the instrument at the animal so I can ward it off and, at the same time, a hand with strong thick fingers wrapped around my shoulder.

With another shriek to make a soprano opera singer proud, I yanked out of the hand's hold spinning around to face whoever was attacking me from behind. My violin slipped from my fingers cluttering on the ground at my feet when the only thing I could see was an arm, a man's arm coming out of a freaking wall. Heart lodged in my throat and mouth dry, I did the only thing I could think of at the time.

"Aaaaaa saaaa!" with the best impersonation of a ninja in the history of the human kind, I even squealed long and loud before executing the perfect chop with my stiff hand over the forearm reaching for me. "Yaaa haaa!" spinning around, I slammed the back of my fist in it, too, and stars burst in front of my eyes from the impact.

"For fuck sake, stop hitting me, crazy female." the arm snarled at me in a deep, whisky-rich tone while I was trying to uncross my eyes.

"Oh my god," I breathed, all the blood draining from my head and pooling at my feet. "it talks…"

The crazy Seraphina didn't kill me, but I will die by a talking arm. That was the last thought before everything turned dark, and I passed out.

Sonata: Chapter Two

Lucien

Muttering under my breath and glaring at the cobwebs stretching across the dark tunnel, I could hear my feet sloshing in the murky, ankle-deep water. Anger was better than feeling anything else, at least for me. Unlike Étienne, who overnight turned into a pushover, doing everything his mate asked, and didn't ask for, I had a plan. With a grin stretching my lips, I tapped my fingers over the pocket of my pants where the rubber earplugs waited patiently to be used. I'll be damned if I allow a female to muddle my brain with her whims.

I neither needed a mate nor did I want one.

What I do need, however, was to get back in the world and search for more information on who the fucker was that killed my father. Granted, there had been decades since his murder, but that didn't mean anything. It only told me that I needed to try harder. Someone, somewhere, knew something about it; I just had to find them. It was only a matter of time; I felt it in my bones. Precious time I was wasting strutting through dark tunnels with murky waters saturated with stench no amount of showers will remove from my skin.

All for a descendant of a Muse, of all things.

My shoulder brushed against the moss-covered walls too narrow for me to pass through freely, and my teeth clenched. My brothers thought I was having the time of my life among the humans, enjoying human females and partying from dusk till dawn. It suited me just fine, so I let them believe it, allowed them to think I've given up. I haven't, and I never will. Our lives were snatched under our noses, and those that sniffled at our feet for centuries were now pointing accusing fingers our way, calling us murderers.

I did not kill my father. Neither one of us did.

But I will go down in history with the highest body count before all this was over.

I will kill them all.

For a long moment, I thought the rage my thoughts provoked was the reason for the red coloring my vision until blues, yellows and greens joined the threads forming in front of my eyes. The pitch-black tunnel, which suited my mood just fine a moment ago, became alive around me within a blink of an eye. My feet faltered, and I stopped my progress, glancing around me in confusion. I couldn't remember if my oldest brother mentioned anything about this before he sent me on my merry way with a dumb smirk plastered on his face. Also, I might not have paid full attention to what he was saying, the presence of his mate messing with my head.

Not like I envied Étienne.

Because I didn't.

"My brother has a mate. A Muse of all things." Muttering under my breath, I scrubbed a hand harshly over my face a few times, regretting it the same second. Shit was clinging to my skin where it brushed against the cursed rocks closing in around me. "And instead of laughing and leaving him to deal with it himself, here I am, squeezing my stupid ass in narrow tunnels looking for another one of those."

The only bright light in this situation was the fact that there was a magic-user in this old building. I might not have control over how things are unfolding in my life right now, but I will take it out on the witch. Killing one of those would surely improve my mood. That idea put more pep to my steps, and I pushed forward determent to see this through before the sun was up. If I deal with it quickly, I'll never have to step foot here or see the female ever again. I'll dump her on Étienne and Moël to deal with, and I'll leave to search for answers on things that matter.

I kicked my foot when something small bumped into my leg and bared my teeth at the damn cat. Melody didn't just insist on coming along like this was something mates did on their daily routine. She also dragged the annoying creature with her, consulting it as if it had an intelligent brain for strategy. And my fool of a brother set back, letting it happen. I'll chew my own throat out before I turn into him. The fact that my heart was thumping hard against my bone and I struggled to keep the hope and eagerness of seeing the Muse behind these walls was not lost on me. Or imagining my cock buried inside her. I just refused to acknowledge such foolishness.

I was a vampire from a royal bloodline, for fuck's sake.

The strongest royal bloodline in the world.

The cat hissed at me, showing its now long fangs as if to warn me. After I healed it, a few things changed in the creature, which I didn't want to examine too closely. Like the long fangs that made it look more feral or the size of it that doubled overnight, along with an occasional blue color matching mine staring me through its eyes. Yet another thing that shouldn't have happened but I had to deal with. All because Étienne didn't know when to stop and take a step back from something he saw as a challenge. I missed the days in court, where all I had to do was listen to words that were whispered in my ear and point my youngest brother in the right direction. It was always the order of things. Étienne was the judge, I was the jury, and Moël, the executioner.

How far the great have fallen. From heirs to the French throne to cowards hiding in the Americas and crawling through nasty tunnels searching for a female descendant of a Muse. The cat bolting ahead and disappearing around the curve in the tunnel made me cuss up a storm. Each word I spat out made me feel slightly better, knowing I don't have to bite my tongue to protect female sensitivities, or Etienne's, for that matter, with the stick stuck up his ass. Rushing after it because I wouldn't leave it past the fucker to think it's a good payback to get me stuck in the murk for hours, I almost tripped over my own feet when a soft melodic voice floated to my ears from behind the wall I was now facing.

"Hey, buddy. You came again." Came the soft whisper pebbling my skin and forcing my fists to clench at my sides. "I missed you for a few days."

With everything in me, I knew I should reach in my pocket and take out the earplugs I brought with me, but like an idiot, I stood there hoping she'll speak more just so I could hear the tone of her voice. Red flags were blaring in my head, but all I could do was breathe and strain to listen to any sound. The creature's shriek of pain made my lips twitch until after a long moment, she spoke again.

"You are imagining things Viola, get a grip." My gut tightened when the tone wobbled as if she was fighting tears. I didn't give a shit about tears that females wielded as a weapon against morons like my oldest brother. "Snap out of it woman, you are your worst enemy. You are hearing things."

A plan formed in my head as I stood like a lovestruck fool basking in her tone. She thinks she imagines things, and all I had to do was scare her more than she already was. If I kept her freaked out, she wouldn't be able to use her powers, whatever they may be on me. Survival had a strange way of making everyone act more on instinct than plan what to say or do next. If I used her fears against her, she wouldn't be able to pay attention to me or any bond that might be tugging at us. With a firm nod to myself, I tried to step closer, and my boot caught on some idiotic rock I didn't see. Cusses spilled from my lips in a long string, my teeth grinding from the sharp pain that spread through my whole foot. I've been stabbed in my torso many times and kept fighting as if it was not more than a graze, and here I was, eyes crossing because I stabbed my toe on a rock. I've never been more embarrassed in my life.

Good thing no one could see it.

Taking a deep breath, I reached with my hand and pushed through the wall that Étienne assured me was an illusion. The strings of colors around me started shivering and writhing like a living thing pausing my movement for a long second. Was it a warning or an encouragement? My brother said he found Melody on the other side of the building, so after her rescue, who's to say that the witch didn't change things? But the fucking cat was gone, so that must've been a good sign. With a harsh glare at the wall in front of me, I punched my hand through it almost to my elbow.

A shrill shriek made me flinch before a menacing grin spread across my face. Étienne was right about the wall being an illusion, and my plan of scaring the female was already working. That was until a sharp pain stabbed through my forearm a moment after the female on the other side shouted "Aaaaa saaaa" with a very strange squeal at the end of each sound. I was ready to pull my appendage back before I lost it when knuckles thumped against my forearm, followed by a shrill "Yaaa haaa." That's when I realized what she was doing.

"For fuck sake, stop hitting me, crazy female." I snarled in frustration, hoping the witch didn't hear all the asinine noise she was making.

"Oh my god," her faint voice came from way too close than I expected it to be, "it talks..."

Not wanting to give her more opportunity to continue with her squealing, I stepped through the illusion into a tiny, barely furnished room with no windows, just in time to see the female crumble to the dirt floor like a marionette with cut off strings. My body took over with a mind of its own, and I had her in my arms a foot before she hit the ground. A jolt of electricity pierced my body, and I dropped to my knees with a gasp, cradling her body to my chest like I've never held anything in my life.

"Fuck me..." the cursed cat was preening and gloating at me from across the room, and I had every intention to skin the creature as soon as I could find my feet.

Sonata: Chapter Three

Viola

Wakefulness pulled me from the clutches of a horrible nightmare where I kept running through a never-ending corridor while large black dogs the size of a pony were snarling and snapping at my heels. Dream or not, I felt my tank top sticking to the skin of my back from the terror induced sweat plastering the fabric to my body. All those things were negligent when I filled my lungs with air, and the most amazing scent I've ever been able to inhale flooded my senses. It was musky and rich, surrounding me like a cloak, and nothing could've prevented the content sigh from slipping through my parted lips. It felt warm and safe.

I felt safe.

Which was insanity all on its own, knowing where I was. The fact that my life was hanging by a thread, and who was holding me prisoner here. I must've lost my ever loving mind, but not even that stopped the feathers tickling the back of my throat or my body responding the way it was, turning pliant and gooey while melting into the firm mattress. Since the day we were locked up in the Chalice, as Seraphina liked to call the cursed church that was my prison, I don't believe I've had a better sleep. Or that the sheets have ever smelled like anything apart from some stinky soap mixed with my sweat from the regular nightmares I had. Come to think of it, I didn't think the mattress was ever this inviting and…cuddly? The same bed with its arms wrapped around my body and its nose pressed to the skin at the back of my ear, inhaling in even, slow breaths.

Memories slammed into my head, making me light-headed. The cat returning, the voice that raised goose-bumps over my skin coming from behind the wall, the arm sticking out of the said wall, and talking to me a moment before I passed out like some dumbass. I might be a scaredy-cat, but a fainter I was not. Praying to whoever was up there listening, I gathered all the courage I could muster and jolted away from those thick, firm arms you'd think someone poked me with a thousand-volt life wire.

"Yaahaaa." I screamed from the top of my lungs, and facing the now cursing mattress with both arms in front of me, I stiffened, ready to do some serious chopping.

"Would you stop shrieking, you crazy female." The mattress that turned out to be a guy, a scorching and drool-worthy guy I might add, hissed at me while electric blue eyes glared at my face.

All my fangirling when it comes to karate movies didn't mean that I actually knew what I was doing apart from the perfect execution of the sound effects if I could say so myself. Those were on point, although not really appreciated judging by the hottie's face that was twisted in an angry grimace. It could've been my stance though, because apart from my hands that I knew were stiff as a board and ready

Sound

to chop his neck, I probably looked like I was trying to pull off a yoga or Tai Chi move. Shaking my head to clear the thoughts, the words that came out of his full lips penetrated my brain with a too long delay.

"Did you just call me crazy, you hott...hot mess you?" I stuttered like an idiot because I almost called him a hottie. *Great job, Viola. I'm sure he feels terribly insulted by your idiotic behavior.* Internally yelling at myself, I watched one of his perfectly shaped eyebrows raise up, the look he was giving me telling me he thought I had a screw loose.

"I am not the one that keeps screaming a bloody murder while someone was trying to come to my rescue." The pointed glare told me I was the stupid person that was screaming the murder in his story.

Anger and fear jumbled my brain and lifting to all of my five feet six and a half inches height; yes, I was counting the half too damn it, I stabbed a trembling finger at his face. "Arms do not come through walls."

His lips twitched at the corners before he sharpened his glare on me. He had no right to look delicious whatsoever while shooting daggers at me through those blue orbs that seemed like they were glowing on his photoshopped face. And just to confirm my insanity, I actually leaned forward and poked his high cheekbone with the tip of my finger, which earned me a snarl.

"Arms don't come through walls," I repeated more to gather my thoughts than anything else. "They also don't talk, and men don't walk through those walls either." My tantrum left me breathless and panting in front of him.

"Good thing I'm not a man." Placing a hand the size of my head on the floor, he pushed himself up to his feet.

"Uhmm..." I had to crane my neck to keep eye contact,

and it would've been intimidating if he didn't say those words. My feet shuffled uncomfortably.

"Ohm?" the line between the brows deepened, and he looked me up and down almost as if checking for injuries.

"It's perfectly fine with me for you to identify yourself however you want. I mean, who am I to judge, am I right?" when his eyes bulged out, ready to pop out of his skull, I kept talking, unable to keep my mouth shut. I always did that when I was nervous or uncomfortable, which at that moment I was both. "I can actually see why you would." I was frantically nodding in encouragement while my hand flopped in front of his nose like a dead fish. "What, with that face and all..." my words trailed off when a deep scary growl started in his chest.

I took a step back.

One moment he was growling at me like some Pitbull on steroids. The next, my back was pressed to a wall, and his chest was pinning me to it. The tip of his nose was almost touching mine, and I felt his breath tickling my skin. Staring down at me, I watched a muscle jump in his jaw like it was the most fascinating thing I've ever seen. And it was, really. This guy perfected the art of grinding his teeth to a whole new level.

"I assure you, little Muse, I am all male." His baritone timbre did stupid things to my insides, and of course, I ignored it as best I could. Which was not at all. Nope, I was doomed as much as I was dumb.

"Huh?" I was sure he knew that his left eye's top eyelashes ended further down his eyelid than on his right eye. They were also very thick and so dark compared to his blonde hair and pale skin, making the blue of his irises stand out even more.

"Are you even listening to me?" hottie narrowed his gaze

Sound

on me, and my fingers were twitching with the need to touch his eyelashes.

"Of course I'm listening." Swallowing thickly in hopes of bringing some moisture to my dry mouth, I cleared my throat. "Remind me again, what were we discussing?" I was pretty sure it wasn't his eyelashes, but I could be wrong.

"Are you drugged?" the scrutinizing way he was staring at me cleared some of the fog clouding my brain, but not enough to make me step away from him.

"No?" it came out as a squeak and a question. "No, I'm not drugged." It was more convincing the second time, but he didn't look like he believed me.

The cat mewled from somewhere to the side. With the guy so close to me and his scent surrounding me from all sides, I totally forgot the poor thing was still in the room. We both turned our heads in that direction. With the movement, my cheek pressed to his, and there was no mistaking the way his whole body stiffened at the skin on skin contact. My ego took a slap in the face, so placing both palms on his firm, muscled chest, I shoved him away from me. He took a slow, deliberate step making sure I know he wanted to give me space and not that I managed to push him.

"What's wrong, buddy?" ignoring the guy and trying to hide my heated cheeks, I kneeled down, reaching my hand to the cat. "It's okay. He was just leaving." Jabbing a thumb over my shoulder at the hottie, I shivered when a deep growl rumbled from the guy's chest.

To my surprise, the cat hissed, arching its back and pinning its ears to his little head.

"It must be you. Animals love me." I snapped at the guy for no reason at all.

The cat hissed again. This time glaring at both of us and flicking its tail as if ready to pounce. I had no time to process what was happening because the hottie wrapped his hands around my shoulders and lifted me to my feet like I didn't weigh more than a feather turning me to face him. Taking my chin between two fingers, he made sure to lock me in his gaze, and like an idiot, I let him.

"Someone is coming." The hottie said, clearing all the hormonal clutter from my head. "I must hide, but I will be back, do you understand me?"

"I might've acted like I'm dumb, but I'm not deaf." Yanking my face out of his hold, I gave him a glare of my own.

"This is important. You can't mention me in front of the witch, or taking you away from here will be much harder. Do you understand what I'm saying, little Muse?"

"Yesss." I hissed just like the cat from frustration. Did he really think I was that stupid? "And stop calling me that."

He didn't look like he believed me, but when the clicking of heels over the hard floors came from behind the closed door, he reluctantly moved toward the wall. Those blue orbs never left my face. The footsteps were coming closer, forcing my heart into thundering in my chest. If Seraphina found him here, there will be a lot of pain as a punishment. She wouldn't even let me see Melody or Harmony. I couldn't imagine what she will do if she found a guy in my room. Plus the cat.

"Let's move, Alto." The hottie snapped his fingers, and the cat bolted across the room disappearing through the wall.

The room spun, and I swayed on my feet. The cat was his?

What the hell?

"I will be back." The guy said once again and melted into the way.

Incredulous laughter bubbled in my chest, and I struggled to keep it down.

"Asta la vista baby." I saluted the air with a snort before the doorknob turned behind me.

Grab your copy...
vinci-books.com/sonata

About the Author

Maya Daniels, USA Today Bestselling and multi-award-winning supernatural suspense author, is a fun-loving woman with many talents.

She traveled the world, gaining life experiences that helped her career as an investigative journalist, as well as her storytelling. Maya writes compelling tales of magic, mythical creatures, loyalty, and life-changing friendships with snarky female characters—much like herself.

Her travels have taken her to Europe, Africa, Asia, Australia, and America. Born with her feet in motion, she currently resides in Ohio, spinning her next epic story that you will not want to put down.

Her biggest 'sins' are her love of chocolate and coffee—through an IV drip! One to never sit still, Maya practices Reiki healing, different types of martial arts, reads about the arcane, talks to furry creatures more than humans, picks up a sledgehammer for home improvement, and travels with her fated mate, seeking her own adventures.

www.ingramcontent.com/pod-product-compliance
Ingram Content Group UK Ltd.
Pitfield, Milton Keynes, MK11 3LW, UK
UKHW040252230426
470297UK00004B/114

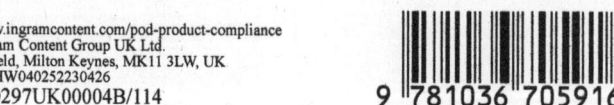